SILVER SKIN

BOOK 2: GODS & ASSASSINS

Frank Kennedy

Dedicated to everyone who enjoys the occasional ambush

A note from the author:

Gods & Assassins is set in the universe of the Collectorate, which includes at least two other series. Reading them is not a prerequisite. However, if you want a wider look at the Collectorate, please check out those offerings. If you haven't read book one of the series, *Red Dust*, please do so before starting here.

I'd love for you to become part of my literary family. Sign up for my newsletter, which drops every three weeks along with free books and special offers. You can also follow me on Facebook at facebook.com/fkennedybooks, where you'll find me hanging out daily. Come on over and let's chat!

1

Nothing roasted my juices like an ambush in the dead of night. Mainly, it was that whole lying-in-wait bit. The one where I watched the victims approach with a shocking level of casual indifference to risk, unaware they were being led to an inglorious and brutal end.

Contrary to popular belief among wannabe assassins, an effective ambush required a fair amount of study and stagecraft. The many considerations included: What were the intended victims' capabilities? Would they adapt to a sudden onslaught, thereby inflicting casualties upon the attacking party? And of greatest import: In what ways might the instigators enjoy the experience?

Killing without a side helping of fun was an empty endeavor, like eating cereal minus the milk. I learned that lesson in my formative years and passed it on to anyone who'd listen.

That philosophy applied to the black hole known as Desperido, where our burgeoning militia prepared to welcome a passel of ruffians into our tragic embrace. These misguided miscreants approached on the one road into town, prepared to send a clear, bloody message: Defying the Horax was not an option.

I finished my walk through the dark town, studied the long-range schematic on my pom, and tapped my ear bead.

"Everyone's in position. Well done, my friends. I expect the curtain to rise on our show in about seven minutes. Hold your ground."

I glanced at Ship Foster, who'd been tailing me around Desperido like an eager pup.

"For all you first-timers," I continued, "Try not to piss your pants. It's difficult to focus on killing a man when your legs are drenched in warm urine. Raul out."

Ship chuckled when I tapped off the bead.

"Good one, boss."

"Nervous, kid?"

"I don't feel a piss coming on, if that's what you mean."

We reached the bottom of the ladder. If not for my night goggles, ol' Ship would've blended in with the pitch dark.

"You've been tapping your pistol for the last ten minutes. Itchy fingers can easily get a man in trouble."

"No worries, boss. I'm on this. I'm ready to do my part."

"Which hand?"

Ship reached for the holstered pistols and contemplated.

"Depends. If it's point-blank, I'm faster with my left." The kid loved his new arm, and why not? Anything crafted out of syneth often surpassed its biological predecessor. "Long range, at least ten paces, I got better aim with the right."

That seemed a fair assessment based on ten days of training. Whenever he fired a pistol, my slender pupil revealed a harder edge than I first observed. Give him a blast rifle?

Shit. He'd be a professional someday. A top lieutenant. A man I'd count on to finish the nastiest jobs.

All that stood between him and a fabulous future was his first kill. That's where tonight's carefully conceived strategy came into play. I wanted Ship to experience the thrill up close. He'd never fully appreciate the transformative allure of murder without staring his victim square in the eyes.

"Climb, my friend. We'd best take our positions."

"Gotcha, boss."

We settled in on the roof of the cantina, the only building in town not shrouded in darkness. I wanted tonight's foul interlopers to see their target from a distance. The old saw about drawing moths to a flame applied.

We watched the drama unfold from a pair of comfy chairs. I threw open three holos. The first showed a gaggle of Horax thugs advance in two sedans, now halfway inside our twenty-kilometer surveillance ring. The second pinpointed the militia's defensive positions – a few on other roofs but some in newly dug cavities my protege nicknamed trigger holes. The third captured a live shot directly beneath us.

The cantina was a hive of unusual activity for two hours after midnight. Twenty good citizens nursed their drinks and engaged in spirited chatter while the showstopper – Lumen herself – played matron behind the bar. She was the object of Senora Evelyn Cardinale's disaffection and thus, marked for death.

As with most things, Lumen did not betray a hint of fear. In this case, with good reason.

Ten days ago, Lumen stopped paying the Horax a weekly twenty-five percent tribute (I gave her no option). Under my incontrovertible orders, Lumen did not respond to outside inquiries regarding her unacceptable oversight.

At that point, Senora Cardinale might have been inclined to send her best men to pay us a visit. Alas, poor Vincente and Mando inconveniently died of a rather repugnant and highly contagious disease which infected hundreds of folks in Machado. Caused quite a stir; its origin unknown.

They never suspected my partner Moon planted the virus through a simple handshake. Nor would they ever.

We framed Lumen for the crime. She poisoned their lentil stew. Truly a shameful example of poor customer service. We made sure the tipoff reached Vincente and Mando before they became incoherent. Did they die with revenge on their lips?

I suspect it was all quite Shakespearean. If you gotta die, bring some melodrama to your last breaths. People remember!

To no one's surprise, Senora Cardinale responded in a predictable manner, albeit a few days later than I anticipated. Just as well: Gave our new militia extra time to prepare.

The Horax were known for nocturnal reprisals. They built a rep on killing folks in their sleep. I respected but did not admire the mercy they granted their victims.

I preferred my targets wide-eyed and unafraid. I wanted to feel their contempt when they recognized my purpose and hardened to their fate. A man who took the time to curse his killer or unleash a good solid wad of saliva made the most of his final breaths.

"Wish I was down there with the action," Ship said, studying my holos. "You sure there's gonna be someone left alive for me?"

"If everyone does their job."

"These Horax ain't the type to surrender."

"You give them too much credit, my friend. They're employees, not martyrs. And they have families to support. When they're deprived of options, they'll extend the game."

The kid flipped up his goggles and rubbed his eyes.

"Here's to hoping, boss. I just want my first."

"And you'll have it, whether on this stage or another. Follow the plan, Ship Foster. Understood?"

"Yeah. Sure, boss."

The kid belonged to me in every way that mattered. Followed orders without question. Until he developed a mind of his own, I needed to handle him with care. Otherwise, he'd get his ass killed. That would be a waste of a perfectly fine left arm.

The sedans dropped their speed and their headlights half a kay from town. I opened a private channel on my pom.

"Seeing this?"

"They're coming in full stealth," Moon said from our little home near the northeastern corner of town. "Like you predicted."

"Eh. An educated guess."

"You think they suspect we're waiting?"

"These folks are assholes, not idiots. Open the shield and let's see

4

how circumspect they are."

A vertical gap unfurled in our perimeter defense, a transparent door opening wide across the central avenue.

"Looks good, my friend. Now, cool your syneth while these pricks make their move."

Moon hated the plan, but not for its strategic inefficiencies. Oh, no. My partner wanted these scoundrels all to himself. Moon argued he was stationed in the perfect position to catch them from behind once they entered town. With his speed, he'd dispose of these disreputable rogues within seconds.

I agreed. But what lesson would that teach our militia?

"Empowerment, my friend. Our army must have the courage to fight *with us*, not stand aside and watch us do all the goddamn work."

Moon imagined lighting a bonfire in the center of town with bodies stacked high. It was an affecting visual, granted, but perhaps a touch too self-indulgent.

Few in Desperido felt comfortable around Moon despite my best efforts. I suggested he ditch the ubiquitous cigar, but that idea proved a bridge too far. Nor was Moon suited for a charm offensive given his lack of said charm. He and I agreed on one potential remedy: The town's fine stable of care workers. He paid them well, and they took a fancy to his considerable skillset.

"Twice a day," I suggested. "An afternoon warmup during downtime and a closer before lights out."

"I'll give it a go, Royal, but I make no promises."

Moon fell back on his original complaint: The more intercourse, the more human he felt. Weaker, somehow.

To his credit, Moon stuck to the routine. Even found one care worker he prized for her extensive repertoire: A tall brunette named Lula.

I stuffed her account with a few extra creds to keep him happy.

"Don't get too cozy, dumbass. You haven't covered all the angles."

Instinct told me to ignore Theo. As usual, my *D'ru-shaya's* timing and lousy attitude snipped away at my joy. Such was his goal.

"Enlighten me, Theo. What am I missing?"

His long, disturbing grunt echoed through my brain like an old drunk burping uncontrollably.

"You know who I mean, Royal. You gave him too much rope."

"Who's that? Vash?"

"He's had two weeks to play along. That bastard's working an angle with his mother."

Vash Rodriguez failed to assassinate me at Lumen's request, begrudgingly accepted my help to repair the very leg I shot up, and brought a team of fellow murderers to town, ostensibly to help train the militia. He had ample opportunity to shift his aim toward me and Moon but settled for sideways glances and veiled threats.

So far.

I indulged Theo:

"I wasn't born in the past thousand years, my friend. I know when a man's biding his time. Vash has a plan, but he won't move until Mommy gives the green light."

Theo chuckled.

"You're not thinking four-dimensional, old man. Vash won't shoot. He knows how fast you move. He'll come through the back door and fuck you through your blind spot."

"Now, that's an image I can't unsee. Thanks, Theo. You're a charmer."

"Doing my part, dumbass. If you go down, I lose my anchor."

Theo assumed I hadn't considered every alternative, which was insulting. However, he lacked access to my human consciousness, so his theories were no more than derogatory conjecture. Or maybe it was the same old song: He was bored and craved attention.

I knew Vash hadn't fallen in line. Ditto for his mother. But at some point, they must've agreed to consider the grand scheme.

Desperido's secret economy stood on the verge of a financial eruption, and a hefty chunk of its success landed in the coffers of their beloved cult, the Children of Orpheus. Dared they undermine the new order? Dared they risk the wrath of a town in love with its newest benefactor? Course not. They'd play my game so long as it suited them – and until time was right to push me off the throne.

Vash passed my first big test three days ago when I asked him to send home most of his eight-person team. Our militia was forty-five strong, fully capable of defending the town, I insisted.

"Your people are better suited helping Orpheus stop busybodies who might expose whatever your group seeks to achieve."

Whatever being the operative word. Neither he nor Lumen cooperated when I gently probed for more information, so I laid off – for a time. My own research – even with Theo breaking off his essence into highly encrypted systems – produced no concrete answers.

Ticked me off.

But like the Rodriguez clan, I too excelled at biding my time.

Vash agreed to send away six of his people. I admitted to a certain relief when they and their tumbler departed town without incident. He blew his best chance to come at me directly.

Now, he waited in a trigger hole on the east side of central avenue, across from the cantina. If he did intend to surprise me tonight, it would happen at the height of our impending conflict. Of all our people in the field, I studied Vash with a discerning eye.

"Any minute now," Ship said, leaning forward in his chair.

The sedans entered the shield opening, unaware of our scan. An array of data accompanied heat signatures on my holo. No sign of any particular vehicle mods. Twelve upstanding Aztecans inside. Eight men. Four women.

Impressive. Cardinale must've been a forward-thinking leader to employ so many deadly women in a male-dominated industry. She earned my grudging respect.

These assholes came loaded for war: Mark 11 blast rifles, a variant of the style used by the Unification Guard during the first Collectorate. These folks were old school, packing thousands of rounds of flash pegs.

"Their ambition extends far beyond Lumen," I told Ship.

"What do you reckon?"

"They're here to take her out then hold the town."

"And anybody who objects ..."

I chuckled. "Long time ago, my friend, the soldiers who carried those guns were called peacekeepers. They did a lot of things, but keeping peace was not their primary goal."

"I heard stories about them. Weren't they monstrous? Like ..."

"Seven feet tall, built like boulders, engineered to hold an empire for the Chancellors. The colonial governments called them in to handle internal conflicts and maintain the so-called rule of law. They did, but peacekeepers used the locals for live-fire practice. As if anyone had the wherewithal to fight back."

"These rifles ..."

"Banned by the current empire. What of it? The Constitution of the People's Collectorate doesn't allow soldiers to drop out of the skies and mop up the riff-raff anymore."

Ship reached for his left pistol.

"We're like the colonials, and the Horax are the peacekeepers."

"Settle down, kid." I appreciated the analogy, flawed though it was. "Yeah, no. There are three things inside those sedans: Big guns, big dicks, big cunts. And every one can be put out of commission with a single laser bolt."

The vehicles rolled to a halt a hundred meters shy of town. I tapped my ear bead for all to hear.

"It's time to play, my friends."

2

C ARDINALE'S ASSASSINS huddled outside the sedans. One spoke. Instructions, I reckoned. They were brief, but the momentary delay allowed me to decipher the leadership structure. The twelve pressed toward town in two waves.

The forward threesome consisted of the speaker and likely his top lieutenants. Nine others trailed by six or seven paces. That group steadily expanded east and west with a rubber band effect.

Interesting formation.

I opened my ear bead.

"They're covering a wide swathe. Not a surprise, my friends. We discussed this potential. Track until I give the order. Raul out."

If the first wave followed a predictable path, our plan would fall into place. However, I couldn't promise we'd escape without casualties; every good general knew the price of war.

"Why walk so slow?" Ship whispered. "Do they know about the ambush?"

"Nah. Whoever's running their operation is careful. He knows to take every precaution, especially when the job appears too easy."

"What if they're tracking heat signatures? That would sniff out our people, wouldn't it?"

"No worries, kid. Scan was clear. These assholes ain't carrying any special equipment. Those Mark 11s are like comfort food."

In their shoes, I'd have felt the same way. High-volume flash peg dispersal was a fine technique for slaughter. It had a track record centuries old. Why mess with perfection, as they said?

Eh. I fought with better. Many years on a battlefield taught me the wonders of a gorgeous little thing called a Force Drum. Large as an arm, and integrated to act as one. It dispensed an energy ball that carved a hole through a man six inches wide. Even the best body armor stood no chance.

Killed me a few times, too.

Those were heady days. I was a simple, bioengineered immortal trying to make his way back home. Died. Reborn. Died. Reborn.

Hell of a cycle.

None of it stacked up to godhood, of course, but there was something special about living in the moment and having no damn idea where the next one might lead you.

"These jackasses are taking their sweet time," I told the group. "Patience will win out, my friends. I'm interested in the three up front. We don't make a move until we have those three in our grasp. Target only the rear guard. Wait for the signal. Raul out."

Ship tapped his feet against the roof.

"You're so calm, Raul. Aren't you worried at all?"

"Worry does a man no good, Ship. I analyze and anticipate."

"But you're not entirely a man. That's your advantage. Right?"

Good thing the kid didn't see my eyes through the goggles. He would've feared my gaze.

"Now is not the time, my friend." He'd been a good boy keeping my secret thus far. "You know nothing of what I am."

"Sorry, boss. I was out of line. It won't happen again."

"Patience. I'll tell you my story when you've earned it."

"Yes, boss."

The first wave picked up its pace. Those three made a direct line for the cantina. They held their rifles at their sides. The second wave entered the killing zone, too, with one dumbass walking within a few feet of the home I shared with Moon. My partner showed considerable restraint, hidden at the bottom of the stairs.

Six months ago, I wouldn't have trusted him to hold his fire. He'd

10

come a long way.

I glanced at the scene inside the cantina. The lively chatter had died, much as one might expect at such a moment. Yet no one made any reckless moves or played their hand too soon.

They understood the necessity of timing their actions with precision and uniformity. Lumen had given up any pretense of going about business as usual. She threw aside her rags and laid a rifle on the counter behind the bar. After thirty years living in the anus of Azteca, she found herself desperately in need of the locals' cooperation.

"One more minute," I said. "Hold those triggers. Hold your breath if need be. I want the lead team inside before you make the first move."

I double-tapped the bead and entered the ears of a new audience.

"Steady yourselves. The door will open shortly. Do nothing until you hear it close behind them. Lumen will provide the cue."

Nothing suited my sensibility more than pure quiet at the vanguard of madness. Even better? To witness it beneath a clear night sky.

"Ship, did I ever tell you I can name every star in the universe?"

"Um, no. They all have names?"

"Oh, yes. Most weren't classified by humans, of course."

"Who then?"

"Now that, my friend, is the greatest story ever told." I leaned over with a big, wide smile. "Earn it. Yes?"

"Sure, boss. I ..."

He didn't finish the sentence. I waved him off with a condescending finger and watched the three badly misguided misanthropes step into the light.

The cantina door swung open. A pair of rather handsome gentlemen – I detected strong breeding in their well-apportioned suits – sandwiched a fortysomething woman with dark red lipstick and a tomboy haircut. I took a fancy to her trench coat and its strong angles. I reckoned she and Moon might have hit it off in another lifetime.

They raised their rifles, and the woman made clear her business.

"Yesenia Rodriguez! I have a message from Senora Cardinale."

How rude, referring to Lumen by her birthname. That must have cut deep. The subsequent message was certain to be loud and fatal.

"Not tonight," Lumen said, delivering the verbal cue.

The instant she raised her rifle, everyone in the cantina stood in unison, precisely as they rehearsed. Twenty-one rifles and pistols challenged three Mark 11s. A fairly even fight.

I expected casualties here. One jittery trigger finger would've introduced a massacre. Instead, we had a standoff.

Nice.

I spoke: "Tell them to surrender, Lumen. Quickly, please."

"Drop the rifles," Lumen shouted.

"You're surrounded," the woman in the center replied. "None of you will make it out of here alive. Be smart."

Enough of that nonsense. I single-tapped my bead.

"Send them to hell."

The pure quiet ended in a cacophonous masterpiece on the central avenue. Not to mention a healthy light show.

Clusters of tiny stars erupted from the Mark 11s in response to the rough linear projectiles of green and yellow laser bolts from positions high and low.

A few screamed. It happened so fast, most of the departed had no chance to contemplate pain or consider the humiliating way their forgettable lives came to an abrupt end.

The holo showed action from every defensive position. Only a few enemy flash pegs targeted any of our snipers' locations.

"Follow me," I told Ship.

We walked toward the edge to view the carnage and account for each of my team. I heard Lumen tell her visitors, "We're not surrounded anymore. Drop the rifles, or we drop you."

Cardinale's chief messengers weren't suicidal. No doubt they sported generous bank accounts and a taste for comfortable living. People often mistook assassins for lowlifes or degenerates. On the contrary. The best ones appreciated the trappings of luxury. Many were highly educated and refined in their pursuits, only one of which was the desire to kill people.

So, after a few seconds of stubborn hesitation, the trio laid down their rifles and on order, kicked them away. I double-tapped to open a channel inside.

"Search them for surprises and make them ready for interrogation. See you soon."

Ship and I stared at central avenue. Our people emerged, walking slowly toward their victims, who lay on the dusty red street in all manner of fascinating contortions. I tapped once and asked everyone to check in.

One by one, they sounded off.

Huh. A hundred percent.

"Anyone hurt?"

A lovely silence followed. Oh, yeah. This was going to be a great marketing tool for new recruits.

I tapped into the town's power grid and flicked on external nightlights for the nearest cluster of buildings. I tossed away the holos and stored my pom.

"Now that is what I call teamwork," I shouted. "Drinks on the house after we conclude our business with these unfortunate creatures."

I looked across to the nearest roof and nodded toward Vash. Now would've been a perfect time for him to shoot me. Guard down, fresh off a shared victory. Why, I'd never see it coming.

He had to be thinking it, but Vash learned his lesson. He'd seen my draw. No, not tonight.

"Why don't you climb down, Ship? I'll meet you at the front door."

"Sure. Whatever you say, boss."

Moon emerged from the shadows and kicked a couple of corpses.

He told the others to make sure each one was dead. If not, end them with a shot to the head.

Time for me to take command. I pushed off gently and leaped. The syneth acted as shock absorbers and allowed for a smooth landing.

"That could not have gone better," I told Moon. "Agree, partner?"

"I'd have done them myself, but yeah. Team effort."

Several first-time snipers gathered around their benefactors. They fit every mold: Young and old, short and tall, gangly and muscular, men and women. Unlikeliest bunch of killing machines a fella might ever recruit. I underestimated the whole lot. As it turned out, many people who lived in holes itched for a change of pace. At the very least, something with a sharp edge.

"Here's where we stand, my friends. I'll head inside and speak to those Horax ruffians. If they have any measurable intelligence, they'll take our message back to Cardinale."

A graybeard slung his weapon over the shoulder and asked:

"What about the bodies, Raul?"

"Exceptional question, Cass. Exactly my next point. Since we've succeeded without having to mourn any losses, I'd like to proceed with the deluxe rewards package."

Amid a confusion of quizzical smiles, the old painter said:

"My brain's a bit hazy right now, but I don't recall hearing that term in the rehearsals."

"Because it's not for you. No. We're going to reward Cardinale with an artistic rebuttal she's certain not to forget. Ilan, you can show them how to arrange the pieces. Yes? A couple of you ought to drive those sedans into town; my partner will lead you through the rest. Congratulations to everyone. I am awash with pride."

They shared handshakes and fist pumps all around.

Nine bodies. People with families who loved them, no doubt. They simply tried to make a living, and never dreamed of being gunned down in a town almost nobody on this planet heard of.

Humans. Out of one side of their mouths: Killing is evil. Out of the other: Well, some folks got it coming. Good riddance.

I loved the hypocrisy. It went down like a nice sour whiskey.

Ship was surprised to see me outside the cantina.

"How did you ...?"

"Took a shortcut, my friend. Now, when we head inside, you hang close and stay alert. I'll giftwrap a little something for you."

His eyes lit up, although I didn't think he caught my meaning. Ship was a bright kid, but the uptake valve was a tad slow at times.

We entered to quite the scene. Our new prisoners were seated and stripped of their outer garments. Behind them, several of Desperido's militia aimed pistols at the back of their heads.

Everyone else raised a glass.

"Well done, my friends," I said to rapturous applause. "You are witness to the fruits of rebellion."

They responded with the requisite cheers. Yep, I owned this town. If Lumen and Vash planned to move against me and survive the coup, they'd best work fast. Their odds for victory were rapidly thinning.

"Now, I'm sure these three fine, upstanding individuals you captured would disagree with my assessment. They'd offer a litany of threats, starting with something along the lines of, 'You won't be so lucky next time. We'll kill everyone in this town.' Eh. No worries, my friends. We have taken charge of our destiny."

Another cheer followed, although Lumen remained stoic. To be fair, she wasn't much more fun than my partner. I cut her a break.

"Outstanding job, Lumen. You're the glue. Never forget."

I saw no outward evidence of appreciation. Oh, well.

"Please, my friends. Feel free to stow your weapons and enjoy the next stage of our program."

Ship and I each pulled out a chair and sat directly across from three people who, in another context, I would've loved to bring onboard. The Desperido militia was a fair start, but I needed stone-

15

cold killers to ramp up the quality of my army. Goddamn, these three were perfect.

I started with a wink and simple greeting.

"Nice night for an ambush. Am I right, people? Clear skies, warm but comfortable. A dry heat, as they say. If you listen carefully, you can hear the lizards screw each other in the sagebrush."

They had no idea who I was, so I didn't mind their indignation.

"It's true. The particular species of lizards that live in these parts actually sing while they make rough and often deleterious love."

I rapped the table. The locals snickered. Though they didn't commune with nature, they knew I wasn't exaggerating.

"I'll begin by answering your preeminent question. My name is Raul Torreta. That information will serve no purpose other than to infuriate you and the matriarch who sent you here. Call me lord protector of Desperido and the vast Naugista Plateau. You could also call me the asshole who made sure you lost many friends and associates tonight. However, I don't have to be the man who sends you into the great forever. Now, it's your turn. Names."

For the record, I never thought they'd answer straightaway. That's not how these sorts of things started. I turned to Lumen.

"Recognize anyone?"

She dangled a rifle borrowed from my considerable stash. Lumen nodded at the man to my left. He seemed a proper fellow with a bushy but well-kempt mustache, black hair greased and perfectly parted from the right. He tried to hide a cowlick.

"Cesar Julines. I sent the tributes to him."

If the man were willing to martyr himself, he might have leaped from his chair. As such, he gritted his teeth and scowled. It was a laughable moment when I considered what Lumen meant.

"The accountant? Lumen, you're saying they sent the accountant in here with a Mark 11 blast rifle?"

Julines pounded the table. I liked a good tough-guy act.

"Malgado," he spit toward Lumen. "After all the Senora did for

16

you. To betray her this way, you ..."

I aimed a pistol between his eyes. That shut him up.

"Yeah, yeah. I must admit, seeing a numbers nerd sporting a Mark 11 is a new frontier, my friend. The fella who keeps the books! Now that is a bold play." I returned to Lumen. "How about these two? Know them?"

"No. I only deal with Cesar."

"Fair enough." I gave them another chance to identify themselves, to no avail. "Guess it's down to you, Cesar. Be a nice guy. Help out a fella, will you?"

He wasn't so smug this time. The accountant turned to the others, whose blank replies told him to take one for the team. Eh. I retrieved my pom.

"Now, let's speed these proceedings along. It's late, and you folks will have a healthy drive back to Machado. I own the best facial recognition tech in the Collectorate. No sense trying to play coy."

The woman grabbed the man's arm. When they shared a deep stare, I recognized their connection. Why did it take so long?

"Brother and sister," I said. "Gotcha. Now, the names?"

"Innes," she replied.

The brother added, "Javier."

"Last name?"

She fought to withhold the answer, which told me what it was.

"Cardinale. Innes and Javier Cardinale. Too old to be her children. I'll take a guess: First cousins."

"What does it matter?" Javier said.

"For you, nothing. But it says so very much about dear Evelyn. Her cousins and her accountant leading an extermination squad. Even the upper end of the Horax hierarchy takes out the dirty laundry. Color me impressed." I focused on the accountant. "Tell me, Cesar. Are you also a blood relative of the great Senora?"

"No."

He spoke too fast. Didn't he understand why I asked?

17

"Good. You simplified my choice."

I handed the pistol to Ship.

"My gift. Use your left."

Ship's eyes ballooned like a hungry diner confronting an endless buffet and wondering where to begin.

"Him? Now?"

"I keep my promises."

He reached for the pistol but came up short.

"I-I should use my own."

"It's a special occasion, my friend. Do me the honor."

Naturally, the accountant objected to the proposed transaction.

"Wait. What are you ...? You can't. Y-you said we were going home. No. Please."

"Hmm. Actually, I mentioned the drive to Machado, but 'you folks' was somewhat generalized, especially where the adjectival pronoun was concerned. Don't you agree?"

Senor Julines started to rise, but a pair of buxom hands caught him from behind.

"Thanks, Harlan," I said. "Cesar, I'm afraid you're not important. She can hire another accountant, but cousins are irreplaceable."

Javier and Innes understood my game: Addition by subtraction. They said nothing.

"Kill him," I told Ship. "All these folks will see your triumph."

"Yes, boss."

Ship gripped the pistol in his left but made a cardinal error (no pun intended): He thought about it.

The kid didn't fire until the well-groomed accountant made a desperate play. Like a smart man falling from a cliff, he tried to fly.

He didn't get far. Ship's laser bolt hit him under the left collar bone. Senor Julines yelped like a little boy and collapsed. Hurt, but far from dead.

"A bit off target, kid. Go around the table. Finish him."

Ship took a deep breath and nodded.

18

I did warn him to temper expectations. Some rookies don't learn.

"No worries, boss. I got this."

That wasn't Ship's voice. It was older, more confident. And the owner didn't give my protégé the courtesy of delivering the kill shot.

3

ELIAN STEPPED OUT OF THE AUDIENCE. Our twenty-eight year-old inventor of Motif, the drug that was going to transform the galaxy in a few years, fired two shots into the accountant's head. He offered me a sharp, reverential nod, holstered his weapon, and returned to his table.

I was torn. On one hand, he showed up the kid. Seemed a little out of character. Those two had developed a brotherly bond since I brought them into my inner circle. On the other, I liked his moxie. Cold, quick, clinical. He demonstrated a harder edge than I'd seen. Oh, and I thought his new hairstyle worked well. Short spikes, platinum blond.

Poor Ship. He returned my pistol and plopped into his chair.

"Don't go taking offense," I whispered in his ear. "Next time, you won't hesitate. Lesson learned."

"Yes, boss."

He seemed contrite, but I doubted his next conversation with Elian would be congenial. No worries. Bad blood shouldn't fester.

"Outstanding. Now that we've set aside the preliminaries and culled our cast to the essential players, we can proceed to the primary business." I asked the audience to sit and relax then reset my attention to the Cardinale cousins.

"First, on behalf of Desperido, I'd like to thank you for exhibiting predictable behavior. I suppose these nocturnal activities follow the Horax playbook, but our beautiful little town is going through a period of adjustment. We're still learning how to fight for our independence and kill anyone who threatens it.

"The best wars are won by the little guys who rise up with great and unrelenting determination in the face of oppression by a larger, more entrenched power."

The siblings didn't betray their indignation, but I heard their mockery just beneath the skin. They wanted to laugh at me, so I beat them to the punch.

"It's damn hilarious to think of tiny Desperido, the ass-end of Azteca, on those terms. We are part and parcel of the criminal element. The rule of law does not apply to our dispute. This means neither side is obliged to resolve its differences by treaty. We will not file our legal claims in city hall. Our war ends with a handshake and a verbal agreement to trust where there is no trust.

"To wit: The Horax and the other cartels will no longer receive a share of the income we generate, whether in the form of tributes or percentage cuts. Their representatives will not be welcome here under any circumstances. If you wish to purchase our products through the normal channels on the night market, you will pay the price we set. It's a fair business arrangement which allows equal access by all interested parties.

"Naturally, we expect you to pass along this message. The Senora is a smart woman. She did not achieve her station without cunning and a head for business. When she assesses the risk-reward of continued violence and extortion toward the people of this town, I'm sure she'll deem the effort unworthy. We could have delivered this message by stream, but we felt a demonstration of our commitment would prove more compelling. I doubt you disagree on that point. So, what say you to our demands?"

They glared at me then each other. Javier tossed a glance over his shoulder, dismissive of our militia.

"I have a question," Innes said. "Who in ten hells are *you*, Raul Torreta?"

"That's not the question, Senora. You want to know how I became the voice of this town. You want to know how I roused these good people to take up arms. Secondarily, you'd love to know where I'm from. You imagine yourself researching my biography and going after the people I care about. Yes?"

She didn't deny it.

"These people might be under your spell today, but it won't last. Desperido will burn."

I rapped the table. "True, Senora. In about six hundred million years, the sun in this system will go nova. Everything on Azteca will burn." The audience chuckled at my pithy rejoinder. "Foolishness aside, let's examine the bottom line. You lost ten people to this town. Twelve, counting Vincente and Mando. The tributes Lumen paid represent less than one-tenth of a percent of Horax income. Your best course of action is to pretend the road ends at Machado."

"All we can do," Javier said, "is pass along your demands. Our cousin does not withdraw, nor does she allow our family's interests to be harmed without appropriate compensation."

"That's what I've always hated about cartels. This eye for an eye business. Good generals know to accept loss and move on to the next battle. You people hold yourselves prisoners to a stubborn code of honor. It only guarantees more blood and more vengeance."

Innes leaned forward. I saw fire in this one. Nice.

21

"You're new here. Yet you took control overnight. Lumen ran this operation for decades. She wouldn't accede unless ..."

Innes zeroed in on the cantina's matron.

"Did he learn the truth? Is he holding it over your head?"

What truth? I wondered. The Children of Orpheus? Her family's ordeal during the post-Collectorate reprisals? Vash? This was another key moment. Lumen could've turned the table. Like her son, she played the game well. She cleared her throat:

"Raul made promises to the people. He kept them. They want him here. I serve *them*, not Evelyn Cardinale."

"You owe her for the last thirty years of your life. That debt stays on the books."

Lumen pointed her rifle toward the corpse.

"Tell the next accountant to take it off the ledger."

"She will never allow this to stand."

Lumen straddled the table before she slung the rifle over her shoulder. Damn, that woman had a way with creating shadows.

"You were still a child, Innes. You know nothing about my debt or the truth. If you did ..."

This conversation turned down an unfamiliar road. I thought Lumen might fill in a few gaps in her biography.

No such luck. She backed away.

"Apologies, Senora, but you'll find no allies here," I said. "Our message is clear. Your cousin will accept our terms, or more of your people will die. It's not complicated. Time to move on."

"And what?" Javier interceded. "You'll allow us to leave, report our losses and your demands, then expect never to hear from us again? In what universe does that sequence line up?"

"The one I control, Javier. Don't think my sphere of influence is confined to Desperido."

I loved bullshitting. It was such a toxic male thing to do.

"You're delusional, Raul. These people have no idea they've been brainwashed. They'll open their eyes up seconds before they die."

22

"Yeah, no. You two were definitely cut from the same cloth."

I pushed back my chair.

"Reckon we're done here. Time to hit the road." I nodded to the audience. "I'd like a couple volunteers to carry out Senora Julines. I did promise him a trip home. Best I live up to my word."

Out of respect for the dead (and for purely practical concerns), I allowed the volunteers to carry the ex-accountant out the front door while the rest of us watched. Ship, Elian, and Harlan took position behind the Cardinale siblings and kept their pistols trained during the next wave of departures.

Harlan was an interesting fella. Thick in the midsection from sitting in front of a canvas most of his life. He claimed to be a pacifist when Ship and Elian first recruited him, but he was actually looking for a spate of adventure. Not much of a contributor to the economy, and I doubted he'd ever amount to much of a soldier. But he offered a nice bridge to the locals who doubted my aggressive strategy.

I pulled Lumen aside.

"That was a fascinating exchange. Anything I should know?"

"I think not. You've opened too many doors, Raul."

"Sleep on it. We'll talk tomorrow."

"You're impossible."

I shrugged. "And relentless. Don't forget that one."

"The Cardinales are right. Tonight won't end it. They'll come at us much harder next time."

"Without a doubt. But not *here*."

Desperido was officially a death trap for the Horax; that was tonight's victory. They still had no idea about the security shield. Ouch.

Those bastards would come at us where it most hurt — in our bank accounts. I looked forward to our next exciting encounter.

The entire militia gathered around a lovely scene on central avenue. The sedans were packed with passengers. Five in each. Four in the back seat, another in the front. All buckled up for the long drive.

Also, all dead. Mangled. Charred and scarred.

The volunteers staged the corpses with aplomb. I didn't want the Cardinales to drive this lonely road unaccompanied.

"The deluxe rewards package," I told Javier and Innes, who stared in obvious horror at their fate. "You'll have a chance to say your goodbyes, reminisce from a one-sided perspective, and show your cousin what happens to outsiders when they enter Desperido. Better still, these souls can be returned to their families for proper disposal. Be thankful. The alternative was a bonfire."

Their snarls suggested they were less than thankful. Although I believe they admired their good fortune at having escaped our town with their lives. They'd no doubt set the Nav to maximum safe velocity. An hour inside surrounded by a handful of late friends and comrades wouldn't impair these assholes for more than a day or so.

"Please, everyone," I said when the siblings entered the vehicles. "Give them ample room to depart."

Some waved, others cheered, a few booed.

The Cardinales disappeared into the thick night, and my partner restored the security shield across the lonely road.

I appreciated the sendoff. This was the first of its kind in my long lives of murder and mayhem. It felt almost … poignant.

"Now that," I shouted, "is Desperido taking charge of its future." Amid the euphoric applause, my eye latched onto Senor Buzzkill.

Moon, who was normally ecstatic at the sight of bodies he killed himself or assisted in slaughtering, contained his enthusiasm like an athlete forced to accept a draw rather than victory.

I stepped aside from the celebration and leaned into him.

"What's your complaint, my friend?"

"None. Your plan worked perfectly."

"*Our* plan."

"I don't think *they'd* agree."

"Eh. Never you mind public perception. That's the domain of the deaf and the blind. I'm the only one who matters, and I know how hard you've worked."

Moon glared at me cross-eyed.

"You think I care about credit?"

"No one enjoys being overlooked."

He tapped my chest with a dagger-sized fingernail.

"Why should I give a damn what these people think about me? I want what I always had with you — fifty percent. And you know what my fifty percent includes."

Indeed. First dibs on high-volume killing. He didn't enjoy sharing the load. I blamed myself. I gave him the green light on those two planets he destroyed. When a man takes upwards of two billion lives, and he can hear their last, wailing screams for mercy, it ain't easy settling into a life of piecemeal murders. The serpent god still had fangs but lacked the same sharpness.

I had hoped the Qasi Ransome job would've satiated those desires. Its effect appeared to be wearing off.

"Patience, my friend. The resupply tumbler will arrive in three days. I have a feeling the outward journey will be more than worth the price of admission."

"Let's hope so, partner. Tonight was a letdown."

I stepped into the fray and settled the crowd for a final word of encouragement.

"It's been a big night for the town, and everyone here deserves proper commendation. That's why you can all expect an extra hundred UCVs in your accounts tomorrow."

I allowed for the cheers to pass.

"But this is one night. The town is secure; not our future. Not yet. That bit starts after sunup. We'll come around tomorrow and record inventory for the next tumbler. We're going to burst records, starting with Elian and triple cases of Motif. Then the fight turns to how we protect our product lines between here and our global and interstellar clients. We know where Senora Cardinale will strike next.

"We'll be ready, rest assured, my friends. But that kerfuffle will dwarf tonight's little affair. So let's celebrate while we can, enjoy a healthy nap, and get back at it first thing."

They understood the stakes. I already told them what was likely to happen after tonight, along with the increased probability for sacrifice. But these people continued to surprise the shit out of me. They broke toward their homes with handshakes, hugs, and a fury no one felt before they encountered us fallen gods.

Vash and Lumen huddled, no doubt wondering how they'd recover from tonight's setback. If our ambush had turned into a fiasco, I'm sure they'd have tried to take advantage.

"What d'ya say we head home and have a long talk, my friend?"

Moon reached for a cigar and sighed.

"Sure. You talk, I'll listen. Like usual."

"Now, who's fault is that? If you tried to be more loquacious, the conversations would achieve an equitable balance."

Moon didn't reply. Elian interjected himself into the moment.

"Thanks for the kind words, boss. I really appreciate it. My guys are working hard to meet our next deadline."

"No doubt, my friend."

"Look, boss. The reason I … I want to apologize if I stepped out of line in the cantina. I don't know what happened. I saw an opportunity and I took it. Ship is pissed."

"He's embarrassed. He'll survive. Patch it up tomorrow. We need both of you at the top of your games. Understood?"

"Yes, boss. Goodnight, Ilan."

Elian scooted away, leaving Moon to shake his head.

"You're boss," he said. "I'm just Ilan."

"No, you're a man with a misplaced inferiority complex. You're sounding awfully, well …"

"Human?"

"Little bit. Could be a good thing."

"Doubt it, partner."

"Eh. Sounds like we need a therapy session. You'll feel better by sunrise. Promise."

I imagined going home, consuming a bottle of whiskey, and listening to Moon work through his various psychoses.

Never happened.

Minutes later, a screaming banshee disrupted my plans.

4

WHEN I TOOK OVER THIS TOWN, I expected Desperido to adhere to its long, boring history where its residents lived at peace in their bunkers and quietly produced goods for export, both legitimate and illegal. I neither carried a badge nor showed interest in settling disputes (except those I instigated, of course).

As it turned out, I was naïve.

The trouble began when Evangeline (too many syllables, so she went by Ev) raced out of her domicile and yelled loud enough for the entire community to hear.

"They're dead! Somebody done killed them!"

Ev didn't stop running until she found me, flailing her pistol as if pursued by an approaching horde. She was an odd bird on a good day, a quiet woman who dabbled in woodwork for a meager living. She joined the militia for the same reason as most: A change of pace from a dull life. Much to my surprise, she scored well in training. Tonight, we had stationed her inside the cantina.

"Calm yourself, my friend. And, uh, what say you holster that weapon before you hit somebody with a random laser bolt?"

She complied. "You have to come, Raul. They're dead, you see. Hortense and Olive. Murdered in their sleep."

My eidetic memory recalled two residents with whom I probably hadn't said ten words. They were part of the biotech enthusiasts, but their product didn't enthuse me. Their vision for scaling it up failed to meet the potential of drugs such as Motif.

"Take a breath and explain yourself, Ev."

She ignored Moon, who stood at my side.

"I found them in their beds, you see. I thought to wake them ... reckoned they ought to know we won."

Everyone not involved in tonight's action had orders to remain home until the morning.

"And?"

"They didn't respond, you see. I had a terrible feeling. Got closer to ... thought I should check their pulse. You know?"

"Yes. And?"

"I pulled back the sheet. That's when I saw the blood." She pointed to the side of her neck. "It was right here where it was done. Stabbed. Got them in the carotid, from the looks of it."

A smattering of others, including Lumen and Vash, gathered around. Here I was, halfway home to that bottle of whiskey ...

Shit.

Many responses ran through my mind:

"They're not going anywhere. This can keep until morning."

"Sorry, but I don't solve murders. I commit them."

"Is there something ugly about Desperido no one told me?"

Alas, Theo hit me with the bottom line:

"It's your town now, dumbass. You broke it, you own it." He chuckled. *"Go play constable, old man."*

It was a fair point, so I didn't waste time arguing.

"Lead the way, Ev."

The gaggle of followers didn't seem overly distressed by this tragedy, which either meant Desperido had a savage edge not evident to the casual observer or this little twist was merely the cherry on top after tonight's massacre.

Ev led us down into her building – House 14 – about thirty meters from the cantina. Like most of these stone structures which appeared forgettable on the surface, it bunkered quite a few people in narrow habitats cut in from either side of a central corridor. It was a far cry from the two-room hovel Moon and I shared.

Lumen told the spectators to remain outside, which was smart given the tight quarters. Ev led me, Moon, Lumen, and Vash to the third cut-in of five on the east side. She shooed away her curious neighbors, no doubt drawn out of a late-night slumber when Ev flew into a panic.

"We'll handle matters," I told them in my most comforting and genteel voice. "You fine folks return to your beds and dream of the profits you'll make on the next tumbler run."

Maybe a tad insensitive, but they wiped sleepy eyes and shrugged. Again, I might have expected them to react with more concern.

Ev's habitat was a typical amalgamation of clutter, with little wiggle room between stacks of cartons, shelves, closets, workbenches, hydrogarden, kiosks, industrial phasic tools, and entertainment pods. She led us to the rear, where wall-mounted light panels cast a blue glow. Clothes hung from metal bunk beds. In between, a tall washing vent with a double sink sported a mirror and several hanging luffas.

Ev pointed to the victims: Hortense on top, Olive below.

The women – both in their thirties – matched Ev's initial description. Their heads laid on blood-soaked pillows, each sporting a small but precise stab wound. Otherwise, they seemed at peace.

"I'm no forensic expert, but I'd say the killer was someone of considerable experience. These women never saw it coming. Wouldn't you agree, partner?"

Moon studied them with a stoic, disengaged expression. He glanced behind and gave the room a once-over.

"Quick and quiet. Yes. Definitely experienced. Carefully planned."

I waited for a reaction that never came. I hated distrusting my partner, but these murders resembled the handiwork of a professional. And none were more exceptional at the artform than Moon and I.

"We need to resolve this matter in short order, my friends. No sense creating an atmosphere of unease throughout the town. We have enough on our proverbial plate, and I want to start taking inventory by noon. Lumen, we can use the town's surveillance cams to narrow down who entered the building tonight, and I suppose we'll need to interview the other residents. Before we do, I think we'd best consider an issue for which I am not equipped."

"Which is?" Lumen asked.

"Understanding who might have a quarrel with these women. You and Ev would know best."

Lumen pushed me aside and took a closeup look at the remains of the day. She threw a hand over her mouth as if trying to stifle her emotions. She bent down beside Olive and mumbled.

"Come again?" I asked.

"I was remembering the day she walked into the cantina. Olive had nothing beyond the clothes on her back." She stood. "Mostly true. She also wore the scars from when her husband beat her."

"How long ago?"

"Five years. Olive said she heard rumors about Desperido and decided to hide here. So, she killed her husband and ran."

"Appears her refuge was temporary. Anyone in town have reason to hurt these women?"

"No. They didn't have many friends, but they kept to themselves — like most of us did before you and Ilan showed up."

I ignored Lumen's predictable broadside.

To Ev, I said: "You three were housemates. You'd know best."

Ev shuffled her feet on a floor badly in needed of sweeping.

"We lived together, you see, but we didn't have much in common. They were close. They done kept secrets. I was what they call a third wheel."

"So, you never happened to overhear anything of a delicate nature? All that time down here together ..."

"No, Raul. I had my own interests. We weren't alike, you see. I carved my totems, and they processed their powder."

Hortense, Olive, and about thirty other contractors focused on what they called "mind and body consciousness modifiers," which was a fancy term for hallucinogens. Their particular powder, which they named Insight, blended with water to produce a clarity of the subconscious, resulting in hypervivid dreams that led the user on a tour toward ultimate truth. At least, that's how they marketed the product. They disguised it in teabags.

Aztecans had a long, storied history of reaching for higher planes of consciousness — mostly through mushrooms and wild herbs — so they jumped at anything making such claims. Consequently, these women generated a fair profit — and no doubt, their income would've remained steady — but the product lacked oomph and risk. It would never achieve the salivating draw of Motif, which created a sustained, full-body orgasm so palpable as to risk heart failure in ten percent of users.

"Perhaps someone wanted them out of business. How many other modifiers live in this building?"

Lumen scoffed. "A few, Raul, but your theory makes no sense. They were not direct competitors."

"That you know of. When did they start making Insight?"

"About a year ago," Ev said.

"Huh. Did they stumble on the idea or learn from someone else?"

"I'm not sure. Like I said, they kept to themselves."

"No worries, my friend. Proper interviews should uncover the truth. Now, you left here for militia duty about six hours ago. Yes?" She nodded. "What were they up to at the time?"

"They sat down to eat is all."

"Didn't seem worried about anything?"

"No, Raul. We just ... well ... OK. We done argued."

"About?"

"They didn't care for my choices." She slapped at her holstered weapons. "The militia."

"What did they say?"

"It was mostly Hortense. She said I'd get myself killed afore long. Said I joined because I weren't making money from my totems."

Hortense might have been right. Ev carved objects worthy of a second-rate gift shop in a tourist district. The hundred-credit bonus she earned tonight amounted to pennies from heaven.

"Must've hurt, Ev. Was that the extent of your discussion?"

"It was."

In the short time since I saw the bodies, my list of suspects grew, and Ev soared to the top. Imagine: A woman who carved wood for a living, who knew her masterful way around a knife, who had a bone to pick with the victims.

Yep. Ev appeared to be outing herself.

Was the investigation going to be that easy?

Hell, no.

"Here's what I propose. No one's leaving town, so we can save the interviews for later. In the meantime, we take these bodies to the phasic trauma pod. It won't bring them back from the dead, but it will scan the injuries and pull every relevant piece of data, starting with time of death. If we're fortunate, the wound might provide clues about the weapon. And the blood panel should tell us if the narrative is not what it appears."

That drew curious eyes.

"What are you suggesting?" Lumen asked.

"Not sure, but it all seems too simple. However, I am woefully under-skilled in the forensic sciences."

I studied each of these four, looking for the tiniest hint of guilt. One of them – or someone acting on their behalf – most likely killed these women. I wasn't a trained investigator, but I also wasn't a dumbass, as Theo often claimed. Three motives came to mind, none a legitimate reason to take out these women.

Then again, who was I to judge? I lost the moral high ground two thousand years ago.

"On the bright side," I told Ev, "you'll have the place to yourself."

She didn't betray her guilt with a little smirk, but I'd bet a few thousand credits that Ev appreciated her new reality. For someone who flew into a panic after "finding" the bodies, she settled down quite nicely, not a tear in sight.

"What should I do with their powder, Raul? They were fixing to load up big for the next tumbler."

"I'll take care of it during the inventory check. Maybe we'll distribute the profits to your account. For pain and suffering, you see."

Ev clasped her hands over her chest as if she were freezing.

"I-I couldn't possibly accept. Why, that's like blood money, Raul."

"It's a one-time deposit, my friend. Then Insight is no more."

"But … hold on. If I found their chemical formula, maybe I could learn how to make it?"

I'd beat this woman at every hand of poker. She violated the number one rule of a murderer: Don't draw suspicion.

I should've pressed her for a confession. Bring this pitiful charade to a rapid conclusion. Could a killer be this stupid?

Instinct told me to back off.

Too. Goddamn. Simple.

"Whatcha say we hold off on property rights, Ev? Let's deal with the issue at hand." I shifted away from the top suspect to the three contenders. "Best we wrap them in their sheets and carry them across the way for a phasic exam. Ilan and I will do the honors. Vash, why don't you clear out the spectators? Lumen, feel free to set the pod for analysis. Good?"

Without objection, we proceeded.

Moon and I encased the dearly departed into as tasteful a wrap as we could, considering the unavoidable red stains. I assumed our exit

34

would be quick and largely unobserved, but Vash had other plans. He ignored my instructions. We passed quietly through a gauntlet of gawkers, perhaps ten percent of the town, before finding Vash waiting outside our destination.

I believe that was his design.

He shrugged upon noticing my obvious irritation.

"They're concerned. They want answers, Raul. I tried, but they weren't about to budge."

He did at least open the door for me.

"Oh, I'm sure they were immovable objects, my friend. You did your very best, without doubt."

He grinned in response to my snark.

Asshole.

Gratitude, I found over these past two weeks, was not embedded in Vash's limited vocabulary. What more could I have done? The man failed miserably at trying to kill Moon and me. In return, we showed our gracious humanity by repairing his leg and trigger hand, both of which otherwise required a transplant.

Moon wanted to kill the bastard, but I often reminded him of Vash's unique value. Our tenuous alliance with Lumen depended on Vash's continued existence. If he died, we'd lose our grip on his mother, and she'd pull support from Children of Orpheus. We needed her cult's protection on the transport routes and their contacts inside both government and the shipping guilds.

For now.

After we achieved proper footing, I had no problem with Moon reducing both to a pile of ash.

Needless to say, the atmosphere inside the medical room was thick with the lingering animosity of frenemies.

"You're to blame," Lumen said while we waited for results on Olive's scan. "Desperido was a quiet town, Raul. You infested it with a disease. You turned these people into killers."

I wanted to accept the compliment but wisely held my tongue.

Soon thereafter, we received unexpected results from the phasic scan. By morning, the security cams created even more confusion.

5

HUMANS LOVED TO INDULGE CONSPIRACY theories, with good reason. Their genetic predisposition toward paranoia lent to the belief that people of means toiled in the shadows, creating all manner of mischief to suit grand agendas. Most theories were illogical nonsense, cooked up by attention-seeking loners and wackadoodles. This allowed the real conspirators to go about their business unnoticed.

I despised these elaborate machinations – unless they involved my handiwork. By definition, a good conspiracy required at least two perpetrators. As such, Moon and I proved ourselves masters of the craft long before godhood. Our two-headed monster reshaped the universes in ways few humans had yet to acknowledge.

Which is to say I was surprised and more than a little pissed to discover a conspiracy had emerged in the town of Desperido ... without my knowledge or consent. Of course, I'd known Lumen and Vash were looking for ways to dislodge us from their lives. However, new data brought to light a potentially more complex arrangement.

The blood scan on Hortense and Olive showed toxic levels of a poison called filamine. It had been in their systems for at least five days prior to their deaths. I knew little about the poison, but research said it derived from the root of the hewpah cactus, which grew on the Naugista Plateau. At low dosage, it induced heavy sleep. Too much at once, and ...

Yeah.

The women died three hours before Ev found the bodies, but what killed them? The poison or the blade? The initial results were inconclusive. Worse yet, Lumen and Vash were genuinely baffled. Lumen even shed a few tears.

"These women deserved better."

"So far as we know," I added. "This seems like a rather excessive attempt to assure their deaths. A double whammy, when either of the two would've done the trick."

"Must be the roommate," Vash said. "She admitted they didn't blend well."

I found myself agreeing with the far less polished assassin, but doubts lingered.

"Ev did seem a bit too eager to claim their formula for herself. If she knew about filamine, she was best positioned to introduce the poison. But why stab them, too?"

"She was impatient." All eyes shifted to Moon, who continued. "She expected the poison to act faster. When it didn't, she panicked. She was afraid of being caught."

My partner spoke from experience. His earliest attempts at murder were often clouded by self-doubt and reckless abandon. His skills required decades of polishing before the ascent to godhood.

Or perhaps he had inside knowledge. How did Ev acquire the poison? She didn't strike me as the type who enjoyed desert hikes in search of rare toxins.

I chose to play along.

"You might be correct, Ilan. It's possible she was emboldened by our takedown of the Cardinale people. In her exhilaration, she chose to finish her roommates and feign shock at their demise."

"They died three hours earlier," Vash said.

"Easy to explain. The poison worked, but Ev didn't know. She assumed they were in a very deep sleep and wouldn't react to a blade digging into the side of their throats."

Lumen stood over the bodies and closed her eyes. Did she say a silent prayer? I'd seen no evidence of religion in Desperido.

"What if we have it wrong?" She asked. "I've known Ev for twelve years. She's a strange bird, and not the brightest."

Vash laid a hand on her shoulder.

"Do you have a theory, Mother?"

"She's not clever enough to develop that poison. But I know who could." She pointed to the corpses. "Hortense and Olive. They claimed their powder induced hypervivid dreams. Filamine induces heavy sleep. What if they were trying to increase the powder's potency?"

How in ten hells did Lumen beat me to the punch? Damn.

"Nice deduction. They introduced filamine into their powder and tested it on themselves. They pushed it to dangerous levels but didn't expect the permanent side-effect."

Lumen replied through clinched teeth.

"I see only one reason why they'd take the risk. *You.* They bought into your promises. They dreamed of increasing their profits, and you were pushing products with high margins. Motif, for one."

Arguing was pointless. Lumen was right.

"I might have inspired them to push the boundary, Lumen. But choices belong to the individual. Some are reckless, and others are measured. You and Vash have had ample opportunities to gun us down. You held those impulses in check to balance your larger needs. Hortense and Olive did not show the same discipline."

They had the good sense not to deny the obvious. Was that a hint of regret I saw in Vash? He scoffed.

"All that aside, we should search their work area and scan their product. They might've introduced the poison into their shipment."

"Smart. We don't want to send a lethal product to market. Motif carries a small risk of death, but it doesn't guarantee a fatal outcome.

39

However, mass murder would not sit well with our buyers."

Lumen sighed. "Whether or not the poison was self-induced, these women were stabbed. Perhaps Ev wanted what they had for herself. Perhaps not."

"If our suspicions are misplaced," I added, "then we need to open a wide net for potential suspects. A killer running amok in a small, insular community does not inspire confidence among the locals."

I shared a moment of glory with Moon, as he too basked in the irony of my twisted humor.

"What now?" Lumen asked.

"Your security system. When Ilan and I moved here, the notion of constant outdoor surveillance puzzled and disturbed us. We didn't understand the paranoia. Now, I believe it's our most useful tool."

I did not remove the old-fashioned monitors from Lumen's office behind the cantina after taking control. Rather, I tapped Bart into its core systems. My sedan's AI prepared a twice-daily report of the most unusual movements through town.

"How many cams monitor access to that one building?"

"Two, although one only captures an angled approach. The other has a clear view of who enters and exits."

"That's where we begin. We'll interview everyone who lives in the building or came and went after sundown."

Lumen's system comprised twenty-six secure cams, none inside. She allowed the residents that modicum of independence, at least.

"It's possible the killer was there all day," Moon said.

"Ilan's right," Lumen added. "I can think of a half dozen who work with contractors from other homes. Some stay the night when the team reaches peak output."

I spent two millennia learning the most tantalizing secrets of the universes. But now? Trying to identify a slasher in a backwater town.

"Don't say it again, Theo. I know. I broke it, I own it."

His devious little snicker echoed through my syneth brain.

I deferred to Lumen, hoping she'd feel more comfortable analyzing the vidstream on her equipment rather than Bart's.

Alas, our time together in her office lasted five minutes.

"It's a glitch," she said upon announcing that cams 17 and 19 had been offline for sixteen hours. "Must be."

"Huh. Now that's what I call spectacular timing. Are the cams themselves defective, or did they lose connection to the network?"

Lumen ran her fingers across a tablet and scrolled through diagnostic reports. A few taps later, the cams reactivated.

"They dropped off. Don't leap to conclusions, Raul. This is not uncommon. I built the network over five years. It's unpredictable."

My side glance at Moon said he agreed with me: Not likely.

"Sorry, Lumen. I'm leaping to conclusions."

"It wasn't sabotage, Raul. See there! Cams 3 and 12 were offline for nine hours during the same window."

"Did they restore connection on their own?"

"Standard auto restart."

"Two points, Lumen. One, secure cams have been around for centuries. No, longer actually. The tech is simple. The odds of an accidental glitch for the only cams showing entry into Murder Central are far-flung. Who has access?"

She whirled around and glared as if accused of leading a conspiracy.

OK, yes. I accused.

"Only three have admin access. Me, you, and Ilan."

"Not your son?"

Vash interjected. "I keep an eye on you the old fashioned way."

"Never doubted it. Allow me to rephrase. Who else do you allow back here to study the monitors?"

"Ship — when he worked for me. He hasn't entered the office in over a week. And he's not likely to have ..."

"Of course he didn't. No one else?"

"No one."

"Then what we have is a miracle of bad timing, or someone here deactivated those cams."

Lumen brushed us aside and returned to the cantina. She and her son returned to my upper tier of suspects.

"Raul, you're a smart man. You waltzed into my town like a force of nature and made it your own. At this moment, you're dim."

"How so?"

"I have wished you dead every day for two weeks. *You.* Not my people. I gave them refuge, protection, and a livelihood. The last thing I'd ever consider is killing any of them."

She'd pass muster in front of a jury.

"Hmm. Very convincing. I like the sincerity in your tone. But we do face a quandary. Neither my partner nor I altered the cams. Most likely, someone is in league with the killer. We lack motive."

"Then you're suggesting ..."

"Yep. Someone else accessed the network. Why and how? We'll need to find the answers. Otherwise, this might be the first chapter in an extended saga of tragedies. In your thirty-one years, how many murders have taken place in Desperido?"

She reached behind the bar and grabbed a tall bottle with green liquor. Lumen flipped over a glass and poured a shot.

"Before you graced our town?" She threw back the shot. "Three. The last was nine, ten years ago. To answer your next question: There was no doubt of the killer's identity. The murders were public. Barfights. A strangulation."

"Did the killers receive justice?"

"Machado's constabulary ignores this town. I sent them into the desert with a day's supply of water. I never knew their fate."

"Creative but fair."

Our initial investigation hit a standstill, and I was in no mood to torture Ev for answers she might not have. She'd keep, much like the corpses we stowed in the trauma pod under its stasis setting. They wouldn't deteriorate until Lumen made a decision on burial or incineration. Meanwhile, Ev had nowhere to run.

"We're tired. It's been a long but productive night. Get a few hours sleep. We'll resume in the morning."

On that point, Lumen and her son agreed.

"Raul, I recommend you hold off taking inventory. The tumbler is three days out. You have ample time. We need to question people. That must be the priority."

I deferred to Moon, who appeared disinterested in either option.

"Will do. One question before we leave."

"What?"

"If Ilan and I solve this murder quickly and quietly, will you do us a small favor in return?"

She dropped hands to hips, her go-to pose for indignation.

"Everything with you requires extra."

"Oh, no. Not at all. You know my favor: Tell us about Children of Orpheus. The group's purpose. What you're planning to build."

Vash spoke for his mother.

"Never."

"That's an ugly word, my friend. All we ask is transparency."

"No. You want us to violate a creed we promised never to betray."

"Think about it, Vash. Talk it over with your mother."

I motioned to Moon.

"Time for bed, partner. Desperido is shutting down."

We walked out into the night with the thrill of our victory over the termination squad diminished.

I had a hefty load of ground to cover before the next tumbler, when this town's viability would be put to its greatest test. After we settled into our bunker and Moon lit a cigar, I chose to gamble on a quick fix. While he blew smoke rings, I analyzed the evidence and came to the only viable conclusion.

"Moon," I asked. "Why did you kill those women?"

6

WHEN MOON WAS SEVENTEEN and not yet immortal, he found me in his father's lab, butt naked in a cell. He disliked me at first, but I saw the kid for what he was: The good son. Trying to do right by his family, trapped on the wrong planet in a worse universe. I knew he'd serve my needs. I convinced him to partake in my escape plan because he trusted me – like everyone who fell for my charm offensive.

He was the oldest of eight children, and Moon cared for the little ones like a third parent. Yet much to my later surprise, and to our long-term benefit, Moon proved himself a fraud.

Killing had become second nature to me, but Moon fought the dark storm inside. He hated the temptations which littered his dreams since he was little. He was one effective trigger away from morphing into a monster.

Good thing I entered his life. Even better, that I walked with him at each step of his journey, able to mold him until he reached the height of his artistry. If poets wrote of such things, they would've called Moon the Serpent God an executioner without peer.

Naturally, he took our great fall harder than me. Without the universe as his bloody playground, Moon went a little nuts.

Well, full-on nuts. Totally, mesmerizingly, and also somewhat pathetically psychotic.

Nursing Moon back to some facsimile of reasonable coherence took years and a patience I found waning. Among the many lessons: I taught Moon to set his sights lower. We'd return someday to the killing business, I assured him. The timeline guaranteed our eventual job assassinating President Aleksanyan's perceived enemies. But the body count might be small, and the jobs few and far between.

Just as he did when I found him at seventeen, Moon adhered to my plan and mentorship.

I sensed minute cracks in our cohesiveness not long after we took over Desperido. Something was off about him in the hours leading up to our Horax ambush, and I sensed it again while we investigated the double murder of Hortense and Olive.

I had little doubt of his guilt when I asked the question, "Why did you kill those women?"

Moon laid back in his bed, expelling clouds of cigar smoke. He stared in silent contemplation. Of what exactly? Did he weigh how angrily he should deny the crime? Did he wait to see if I was serious? Was he prepared to accuse me of betraying our endless friendship? Or was he searching for a witty retort? A touch of snark?

No sane mortal man would've asked the question unless Moon was trapped in a cell or restrained. Between the thick, full beard, the hair running halfway down his back, and those deep, dark eyes – let's just say there was no mystery as to why he intimidated the locals. He was so far removed from the sweet, well-groomed Hokki teenager I met all those eons ago.

"Remind me again," Moon replied. "What were their names?"

Ah. So that's the game he wanted to play.

"C'mon, my friend. You didn't choose them at random."

"Sure about that, partner?"

I reached for that whiskey I'd been hankering for all night.

"Two hours before the ambush, you walked the town, making sure

45

all the non-combatants were tucked away in their homes. It would've been nothing for you to duck inside and jab those two in the carotid. At full speed, you would've been perceived as a blur to any witness."

Moon scratched his beard.

"That's a solid theory, Royal. The timeline fits, and next you'll remind me that I had access to the security cams. You make it seem nearabout open and shut."

That first gulp of whiskey soothed my innards.

"You have an alternative theory, my friend?"

"Would it make a difference?"

"I love clever. If you offered an intriguing story that matches the timeline, provides a lock-solid motive, and fills cracks before they open ... I'm game to almost anything."

Moon crossed his legs and pointed to the unopened bottle of Mesquine rum on the counter.

"Toss it to me." When I did, he caught it with one hand. As he twisted off the top, Moon continued: "I have a theory. Do you want to hear, Royal? It's very clever."

"With bated breath, my friend. Tell me."

He sniffed the rum and hesitated. Likely, he adjusted his olfactory sensors. Then Moon swigged the rum, screwed on the cap, and set the bottle aside.

"Here's what I believe happened. About eight days ago, those women – Hortense and Olive – received a hundred-gram package with ground root from hewpah cactus. It probably included instructions on how to derive a ten milligram dose of filamine and blend it with their drug to produce incredible dreams.

"But I suspect there was an error in the instructions. The numeral ten was missing a zero. Unfortunately, they blended a hundred milligrams into each batch of Insight. They were desperate to improve their product, but they couldn't send it to market without testing it. And there wasn't time to ask for volunteers."

He pulled on that damn cigar with a calm, cool discipline.

46

"They started slow to judge the effects. Every night, they upgraded the dosage. When they woke refreshed each morning for the first four days, they discussed their dreams and knew they had a true winner on their hands. They stopped taking the drug and focused on production. But they didn't know filamine lingered in the nervous system for days. They didn't understand what it did to the synaptic bridges in the medulla oblongata.

"They went to sleep tonight, and their system ... shut down. It was a peaceful death. *I assume.* Also pointless. Never knew they were in trouble. Never felt fear or pain. Their roommate wouldn't find them for hours. After analysis in the trauma pod, we'd conclude that they died of an overdose. A waste, don't you think?"

Moon spoke in a deep, contemplative voice. He sounded like someone who carefully took stock of the bigger picture. That wasn't the man I knew.

"I agree, Moon. A waste. I wonder, though: What would be the point in someone hiding the overdose with a knife to the neck?"

"Oh, I'd assume the killer wanted a more dramatic scene. Humans are easily panicked."

Point taken, but there was one missing component.

"I question how the killer knew Hortense and Olive had expired."

There it was: A slight upturn of the lips. The hint of a grin.

"An educated guess, Royal? I think the man must have interacted with these women at some point. He touched them and transmitted a blood tracker through their skin. Perhaps he linked the trackers to his pom and received a notification when their hearts stopped beating. Perhaps for the first hour, he was satisfied. Then as he walked through an empty town waiting to ambush a team of killers, he grew bored.

"Maybe, Royal, he wanted a small taste of fun before the main event." Moon expelled a narrow stream of smoke and reached for the rum. "Of course, it's all just a theory."

Wow. The face of a serious man who chose his own rogue course this time. I should've been proud, for this surely was the next stage in his growth. Yeah, no.

"Intriguing, Moon. The killer chose to shift blame from overdose to framing the roommate. Did he hold a grudge against Ev?"

"Nah. I doubt this man begrudges anyone. He enjoys the sport. But I suppose he watched the roommate while she trained for the militia and thought she'd make an easy mark. Uneducated, slow to grasp anything other than a knife and a rifle. But competitive. Definitely competitive. Just the sort who might think she'd use their chemical formula to build her own product line."

As he swigged rum, I held out my whiskey bottle in respect.

"You disreputable piece of shit."

Moon wiped his lips.

"Thank you, partner. That means more than you know."

"Now, let's return to my original question. You haven't answered. Why did you do it, Moon?"

He uncrossed his legs and leaped from the bed, bottle in one hand, cigar tucked between his lips. He set the rum on the counter and expelled smoke through his nose.

"Royal, do you remember our last night in Bessios? The Corral?"

Our last great adventure as immortals before we ascended.

"Nineteen hundred and thirty-two years ago on the standard timeline. Could've been last week."

"Or ten minutes ago. It lives with me. Do you know why?"

"Tell me. Please."

"Because it was the single greatest day of my lives. You molded me for sixty-three years until I reached the peak of my craft. I remember every Destroyer whose head I sliced away. We were covered in their blood, standing among dozens of headless corpses. Victors. We went where no immortal dared.

"I looked at you and said, 'We're not human anymore, are we, Royal? We're monsters.' Remember your reply?"

A beautiful moment indeed.

"I said, 'All humans are monsters. Some just lack the training.'"

Moon grinned.

"You gave me the gift I craved but never would've had the guts to grab on my own. I was a warrior, relentless and cold-blooded, armed with the skills of a master. I knew how to kill without mercy. And I wanted more."

"All of which you took, and then some, after we ascended."

He wagged a finger in my face – not a gesture I appreciated.

"There was no end to it, Royal. Not my desire, or the number of my victims. I wanted to jump from universe to universe, choose the next slaughter, and feed my hunger to the end of recorded time. You were at my side. You enjoyed it. Hell, you celebrated it. You egged me on."

"Yes. And then we had to sacrifice our fun for the greater good."

"Did we?"

"For the humans? For what was left of our moral compass? To change reality itself? You're goddamn right we did. You agreed, Moon. You were fully onboard. I must've asked a thousand times. Never once did you hesitate."

"Because ..." He pressed his face into mine. Oh, I was not a happy camper. "I was having the time of my lives. I didn't understand how miserable I would be in this form again."

I pushed cigar-face away.

"And it cost you several years of sanity. But I kept my promise, Moon. We're on track to fulfill our goals. Another year and ..."

"A year of playing nice. Training, administering, and tolerating these humans. I need more. I need it now."

I stifled a laugh. We covered this ground before, but his passion felt deeper tonight, his turbulence unprecedented.

"My friend, I gifted you two hundred innocent humans last month. We shared kills at the fort, we obliterated Vash's team, and tonight we inaugurated the first pieces of our army into action. Many more will fall in three days. You'll have sufficient blood. It won't be on a

49

planetary scale, but those days are done."

"Then why can't I leave them behind, Royal? Why do I feel like I'm debasing myself in this miserable little town?"

"Huh. *Debasing*. I haven't heard you use that word since the day we met. You accused me of debasing myself by undressing in your father's cell."

"That has nothing to do with ..."

"Disagree. It might be everything. Lessons learned, at the least. We were human then. We survived by defying laws laid down by conquerors. We outmaneuvered the Swarm. Our escape was a modest victory. But the laws of the universe caught up with our asses. Only through luck and circumstance did we find a second chance outside of time."

His eyes narrowed into slits, a sure sign of dwindling patience.

"What in ten hells is your point?"

"There will not be another second chance. We live under *their* laws. We abide by any systems we can't circumvent. We make our fortune and work to hold it. We might be stronger than mortals, my friend, but we ain't invincible – as I've told you more often than I can count. Patience. Discipline. Restraint. Without them, we'll find ourselves in a crater of shit so deep we'll never dig our way out. Killing those women was impatient, undisciplined, and reckless."

Moon's rage settled and his eyes softened.

"It brought me pleasure, Royal. Think about it. I was patient. I developed the plan ten days ago and allowed it to play out. I was disciplined. I gained my victims' trust and passed the blood tracker without their knowledge. I showed restraint. I didn't attack until I knew they were dead and there'd be no witnesses. I circumvented security and did my part when the team needed me. I never placed us at risk."

Son of a bitch. Moon demonstrated the hand of a mastermind. Why wouldn't a best friend be proud?

Eh.

"Now that, dumbass, is what I call a takedown. You should hear Addis cheering. She's all about the hero worship."

"Please, Theo. Close the door and give me the room."

"With pleasure, Royal."

"How do you expect this to end, Moon? Two women are dead, and I can't pin it on you."

He shrugged with an ain't-it-obvious demeanor.

"You'll find the blade under Ev's mattress. It's her favorite carving knife. Only *her* prints. You'll find their last eight days of lab notes next to the knife. I removed the instructions for deriving filamine and the hewpah roots I gave them. It was forty-two seconds of work."

"She'll proclaim her innocence when she's accused."

Moon grunted satisfaction.

"The evidence will speak louder, Royal."

"What of the secure cams?"

"A glitch, just like Lumen said."

"And her sentence?"

"I don't care. Let the town vote. Choose between firing squad or desert exile on one day's water. Then it ends."

"For how long, Moon?"

"That's up to you, partner."

"Explain."

He approached like he was the ex-god in charge.

"Accelerate the timetable. Get us out of this town. Give me equal partnership in all things."

"This town saved our lives. If we had remained at the fort ..."

"We can work from anywhere in the Collectorate."

"We have the makings of some fine soldiers."

"A handful. Ship. Elian. A few others. The rest? Are you kidding?"

I needed a whiskey-on-whiskey breakfast. I felt like a man who owned fifty-one percent of a business, and somedamnbody was trying to steal one percent. So ungrateful.

"You're afraid, Moon. That's the real problem. The *why* you refused to disclose."

"Afraid of what?"

"Losing what you became that night in Bessios. You feel your humanity rising. It's fighting for a place alongside the Destroyer."

"Bullshit, Royal."

"No. I dealt with it years ago, while you battled insanity. While I nursed you back to health. Without that humanity, I would've incinerated you and moved on alone. But it killed me to see you suffer. You have been my brother, for better or worse, going on two thousand years. We are the only two of our kind in existence. In saving you, I found a balance between the god I wannabe and the man I have to be if we're going to build our empire. Are you hearing me, Moon?"

I honestly never expected to make that confession. The words assaulted me before I could repel them.

Damn. Being human carried far too much baggage.

Moon retreated to the rum. He drank a quarter of the bottle and licked his lips.

"I hear you, Royal. I always have. I know what you sacrificed. But I am half this partnership, and you will treat me with equal footing. I will *not* follow. I will co-lead. And my demands will not change. Leave this town. Accelerate our timetable. Allow me to choose my targets on my own terms."

"If I refuse?"

"There are six hundred and two humans in town. The number will drop faster than you expected."

He spoke with the calm of a man who found clarity. I hated those kind of people – they were the most dangerous.

"Moon, I'm gonna ask you a question I never imagined would cross my lips."

"Good. I'm tired of hearing the same old shit from you."

I took a deep breath and played a hunch.

"When was the last time you wanted to kill me?"

52

The answer was slow to come.
It would've broken my heart, if I had one.

7

Resolving the double-murder case that morning would have satiated Moon and created the illusion of acceding to his demands. Instead, I used my most effective tool to buy time and keep our humble little town on track for its next showdown with the Horax.

I showered friend, foe, and follower with the pacifying words they wanted to hear.

To concerned citizens: "You not need fear a repeat of last night's unfortunate episode in House 14; matters are well under control. Focus on assembling your product line for our most lucrative inventory."

They smiled at the idea of greater profits, but even a charismatic and staggeringly handsome man like me couldn't hope to assuage their concerns. Humans didn't abandon fear or gossip overnight.

To Lumen and Vash: "I've reconsidered, and I now believe the security cams glitched. My humblest apologies for suspecting a conspiracy. I'll conduct a quiet investigation and resolve it before the tumbler arrives. Lumen, why don't you organize a wake for Hortense and Olive? Drinks on the house. I'll buy."

She didn't sneer, which I considered progress. She had to know I was playing an angle. Vash was surprised when I offered him a more vital role in our affairs.

To Ev: "You should leave while we conduct an investigation. Take your essentials to House 25, Cube 4. They have a free bed. I'll compensate you for whatever losses you incur if your product line isn't ready for shipment."

Ev asked after her late roommates' powder, which might have enhanced my suspicion if I didn't know better. She was disappointed to hear it would be impounded and ultimately trashed. But she gathered her personals and quietly moved. I put her up with two other members of the militia. One less point of tension.

To my partner: "I have no objection to co-leadership. Take full control of the town's security and refine our plan for the tumbler. Vash will be your second in command. Tomorrow, in order to split the load, I'll segment the town for inventory. We'll each take half. I'm afraid this will involve both administrating and tolerating, which you apparently loath, but it will expedite our next move. Who knows? They might even start calling you 'boss' as well."

He didn't whine or object, per se. But he thought the price tag for leadership seemed a bit steep. Only when I suggested the work might be too complex for him, did Moon relent.

I did not consider it a victory, moral or otherwise. Moon's disquiet had been building for longer than I suspected. I recounted many conversations over the past several months; the clues were there had I been willing to listen.

Such was my morning.

While I left those concerns spinning on plates, I ventured to House 34 to deal with a surprising issue that arose during the Cardinale interrogation. Ship joined me, still livid about having his big moment stolen by Elian.

"There's no point assessing blame," I told the kid. "He finished the job where you came up short."

"I hesitated, boss. That's all. If Elian hadn't stepped in, I would've killed the accountant. He embarrassed me in front of everyone."

"Not his intent, and I can't have you at each other's throats."

The kid seethed. His eyes appeared to burrow inside narrow white slits when he was well and duly pissed. I loved his passion and decided on a resolution. His anger morphed into anticipation at my proposal.

"Really, boss? No consequences?"

"Not at all. It's a fair response. I'm sure Elian's man enough to handle the blowback."

Ship balled his fists when we entered House 34, the center of Elian's Motif production. His associates occupied four cubes. They sacrificed living space to expand the lab, work benches, and product storage.

Per our plan, I entered Cube 7 and told Ship to wait around the corner. Give me two minutes, I insisted. The kid smiled.

I doubted he would hesitate this time.

Elian raised his goggles over his head when he greeted me.

"Morning, boss. Come around to check on progress?"

"Among other things."

He pointed to the silver cases at the far end of the lab.

"When we heard you'd put off inventory until tomorrow, we decided to run another line of wafers. That's eight hundred more."

"You expect how much altogether?"

"Ninety-three hundred."

"Nice." I ran a quick calculation. "You and your team should gross close to half a million UCVs, including residuals."

Elian pumped his fists.

"That's just the prelims, boss. Once we expand ..."

"People used to say, 'The sky is the limit.' I do believe interstellar shipping has rendered that old saw moot."

"My team is fired up. I've had twenty inquiries about joining. We're all the rage."

"Look at you." I tapped Elian on the back. "A full-fledged man of business. And to think, no one in the biotech industry so much as gave you an interview. You've come a very long way, my friend."

"Thanks, boss. That means the world to me."

"Actually, I wonder if I might borrow you for a couple of hours. We'll be spending it on Bart."

Elian beamed. I had taken him for a test flight a week ago, when I allowed him to handle the manual Nav for a few minutes. He became a science nerd in heaven.

"More flight training?"

"And a well-earned surprise."

"Sure, boss. Anything for you. I'll ask Renaldo to take over."

The next bit happened according to script. I have to say, Ship played his part to perfection.

When Elian turned to call for Renaldo, his right-hand man, Ship blew past me, swung the taller Elian about and kissed him with a blistering right hook. I thought I heard a pop before Elian stumbled backward, hand over his left eye, and fell into an unoccupied bench. Work in Cube 7 ground to an instant halt.

Ship stood over Elian, both fists prepared to continue a thorough pummeling. However, the kid lost his advantage after the swing I allowed. When Elian – four inches taller and far more dangerous than I believed anyone in town understood – regained his bearings. A gentleman would have accepted his comeuppance in that moment. Elian wasn't quite there yet.

He lunged at the wiry kid, but I intervened.

"Settle please. Both of you."

"Boss," Elian insisted, "he suckered me! I can't ..."

"Let it go. Yes. You can and will, Elian. Ship, stand down."

I waited until their testosterone cooled.

"Elian, I asked you to make amends with Ship this morning. Apparently, you forgot. In the spirit of fair play, let's agree you deserved a healthy smack as retribution for last night. Ship, you made your point. Now, we need to consider the ledger balanced."

Elian winced as he touched the red area around his left eye, which he shut. Ship had not only found his target but delivered a smashing blow. The kid was coming into his own.

"You are two of my most important lieutenants. I have huge plans for you both. But you must understand: I will not tolerate dissention in my ranks. You do not have to be friends, but you *will be* brothers in arms. You will carry each other's lives in your hands for the dangerous times ahead. Do you object to my terms?"

"No," Ship said, rubbing his sore right hand. "I'm with you, boss."

"Same," Elian added. "You're right. Guess I had it coming." He extended his hand to Ship. "I wasn't trying to show you up."

They shook like gentlemen, more or less. I doubted the incident would be permanently shelved. Still, I enjoyed seeing friends make up over a case of who should've killed whom.

"How's the eye?" Ship asked.

"I can still see."

"We'll run a diagnostic on Bart," I said, "but I suspect your ego suffered more than your eye."

"Yes, boss."

"Ship, now that you've achieved satisfaction, please report to Ilan. You'll be working alongside him and Vash today."

"But I thought we ..."

"Plans have changed. You'll help with inventory tomorrow."

He turned down his chin.

Eh. Angsty teens.

After Renaldo stepped in for Elian, my very own drug kingpin and I proceeded through town. Elian comported himself in a weathered black trench coat, which complimented his dark sunglasses and provided a nice contrast to the spiked blond hair.

He wore a tattoo of the double helix on his neck, barely visible above the collar. Experience told me not to trust anyone with a neck tattoo, but I gave Elian a pass.

For now.

"Boss, I have to ask a question," he said as we approached Bart.

"Did you set me up back there?"

I chuckled. "Just now reaching that conclusion, are you?"

"Why, Raul? Ship and I could've sat down and talked it out. We had a misunderstanding, but we're friends."

"He's a boy. You, Elian, are a twenty-eight year-old man. It was your responsibility to seek him out, as you promised me. Until Ship becomes the man I'm grooming him to be, you will take the high ground. Every. Single. Time. Yes?"

We paused outside my Ladybug class sedan.

"I get it, boss, and I'll do better. I don't mean this to sound like an excuse, but I've never been good at apologies. You might've noticed, folks in Desperido don't have top-notch social skills."

"I knew that before I set foot in town."

"Oh. Our reputation precedes us?"

"No, but four misguided thieves did. Time to board, my friend."

I skipped the phasic diagnostic on his eye and offered him the copilot's seat. Elian removed his sunglasses, settled into the comfy chair, and sighed like a techno-geek might post-masturbation.

This man showed a fearsome love for Bart. He learned all the features (including those for which I swore him to secrecy) and knew the textbook history of the Ladybug class and its predecessors. The first time he took the controls, Elian rambled through the entire flight about how he had intended to be one of the UNF's top navigators before he failed the entry physical.

On that day, I appreciated his enthusiasm because I shared his affection for my customized turquoise beauty. Yet I also pitied the fella. How can you not feel bad for a victim of shattered dreams?

Actually, it wasn't as hard as one might think.

"Take her up, Elian."

He launched the terrestrial Nav holo.

"Where to, boss?"

"Thirty degrees southeast over the Plateau about two hundred kay then swing west for a bit. Low altitude, moderate velocity. After that, we'll try something new."

I caught his gasp of excitement. His lack of a reply said he didn't want to jinx his good fortune.

After a smooth departure, he surrendered control to the AI. I grabbed the whiskey kept nearby plus a pair of glasses.

"Do you have a favorite drink, my friend?"

"My stomach's made of iron. I drink whatever the host offers."

"Savor this one. Small sips. Trust me."

I poured him a double just to see how well he listened. Elian's eyes swelled upon first sip. The heat blindsided him.

"W-what is this?"

"A little something I picked up on a business trip to Hansen's Landing." Moon and I killed three targets during the two-day visit. "The natives call it easter eye whiskey. A hundred milliliters will set you back ten UCVs."

He studied the bottle and dropped his jaw.

"So you spent ... two hundred creds?"

I shrugged, as if the expense were nothing. Actually, I acquired it off a dead man.

"These little luxuries are pleasant reminders of what it means to be successful, Elian. Any businessman worth his measure will indulge in a modicum of excess."

I left him to dream of a grandiose future when he might afford such amenities. I scanned the desolate red desert before us and zeroed in on my home of nineteen years. From this vantage, the crater that was once the Fort of Inarra went deeper and wider than I had imagined.

Whoever jumped out of a wormhole eleven days ago and destroyed it made sure the effect was total. None of the thousand-year-old structure stood. Had we been living there, I doubt our speed would've allowed us to clear the blast zone in time.

We agreed that night to downplay the explosion, which drew the eyes of many in Desperido. Some wanted to investigate, but we said

Bart tracked a meteor impact in that area. To my pleasant surprise, it drew no attention outside the region. I didn't expect our luck to hold out much longer. A satellite was bound to discover the anomaly.

Elian didn't realize what we flew past, which was just as well.

"Raul, I gotta ask: How many creds have you put into Bart?"

Nope. Any specifics would generate nagging questions about how I achieved my wealth. I could've spun ample tall tales for my curious lieutenant, but this little sojourn wasn't about me.

"I buy tools to enhance my life. The price stamp is unimportant."

"Hope I can say the same someday, boss."

"On your current track, there's a high probability."

Elian took a cautious second sip. He scrunched his lips but downed the liquor with more aplomb.

"I try not to think about it. Being rich."

"Why's that?"

"It always felt out of reach. We didn't have much when I was a kid. When I washed out of the UNF and couldn't find a respectable paying job … fuck. After moving to Desperido, I got used to the idea of living out my life in a hole in the ground."

"Many in town feel that way, which I find astounding. Not the part about escaping from society. A quiet place offers many benefits. But as a permanent solution? No. Desperido is an early grave. A lazy answer to complex problems."

Bart veered on a more southerly trajectory to the wide-open heart of the desert.

"I'd just about given up when I created Motif. The whole concept was so damn perverted, I wasn't sure it would sell."

"That's because you don't understand humans, my friend. Personal happiness is the number one priority, regardless of what the most selfless claim. What greater sensation than the ultimate orgasm? Yes?"

Elian cracked a demon's smile.

"Sure enough. I tested it before I sent it to market. The real thing

61

can't compare. But one shot was enough for me."

"Oh, yes?"

"I knew if I tried it again, I'd never stop. Would've been dead within a month."

"You understood the inherent danger."

"Everyone on my team, I tell them: You get one free shot. Come back for more, and you're out the door."

We began steering down the road I needed him to pursue.

"You're not afraid they'll steal product. You want them to live."

"They're my friends. Sure."

"But you have no problem sending a drug to market that will surely kill some of it users."

Elian studied the golden liquor.

"You said it yourself, boss. Individuals make choices. It's not my fault if they play roulette with their lives."

"No, it's not. And if it wasn't Motif, they'd latch onto something else equally as hazardous. However, I doubt we'd need a solicitor to make the argument that because you know the drug will kill roughly one in ten users, you are a murderer. And as Motif's range and popularity grows, you will by extension become a mass murderer. How do you feel about that assessment, my friend?"

For a moment, I thought his bronze skin turned a shade of off-white. In my experience, the best drug manufacturers shielded their conscience from a whiff of guilt by simply pointing to the pleasure and/or relief they provided the consumer. Thus, I found Elian's response predictable.

"Everyone dies of something, boss. People who use Motif die with a smile on their face. That's a gift."

I tossed back the rest of my drink and set aside the glass.

"Well said, Elian. I'm pleased to know you're steeled against what lies ahead."

"What do you mean?"

"I believe we can scale your product to such a level, it will be accessible on all forty planets within three years. At end of five, we'll have bases of operations everywhere. A hundred million people will use Motif per annum. If the statistics hold, that should mean roughly ten million deaths. Can you live with that future, my friend?"

He stopped the glass shy of his lips, swallowed hard then finished his drink. Elian wiped his lips with his tongue.

"We'll make billions, right?"

"Oh, yes."

"Then yeah. I can live with it."

Nice.

Other than a pair of fallen gods, I doubted few humans would express that view without hesitation. It confirmed what I thought about Elian in the cantina last night.

I reached inside my jacket and grabbed a pistol. I laid it in my lap, the barrel pointed toward the copilot.

"I'm an ambitious man. Desperido is a temporary divergence. I have a town to run and a future to build. I thought you'd be a major part of it, my friend, but now I'm less than certain."

He stared at the pistol, paying no mind to the Nav for the first time since we took off.

"Raul. I d-don't get your meaning. What did I do wrong?"

"You've been lying to me, Elian. To all of us."

"No. I ... what ... about what?"

"That's for you to reveal, my friend. Truth will be worth billions. Falsehoods, on the other hand ... well, let's just say you'll wish you were riding high on Motif."

My discombobulated lieutenant dropped his empty glass.

8

FEW THINGS SATISFIED ME MORE than watching folks squirm. They didn't necessarily have to be staring into the face of their impending death, but it heightened the drama. As such, I milked these sweet little moments – sometimes long enough to watch grown men piss their pants.

Not today. Elian deserved better, so I cut to the chase.

"Last night, you revealed a side of yourself heretofore unseen. It's not that you killed the accountant and embarrassed Ship. I've already forgiven your indiscretion."

"Then what did I do wrong, boss?"

"In my long travels, I've learned to see into a man's heart based upon how he takes another life. You might say I'm something of an expert on the subject. The way you comported yourself – quick, cold, and efficient – told me you are accustomed to killing."

I saw Elian's confusion. He looked toward me but not *at* me. He debated whether to come clean or deny it up and down. Which one did his boss want to hear?

"Raul, I haven't lied to you or tried to misrepresent myself."

"Yeah, no. See, lies are dicey. There's the blatant falsehoods, and then there are the many omissions. I don't intend to debate ethics, Elian. But your backstory is leaking air."

64

Elian recovered his glass and pointed to the bottle.

"Can I have another shot, boss?"

I accommodated. He swallowed it in one gulp.

"You told me your life collapsed when you failed the UNF physical and received no interviews for biotech jobs. You claimed to have been treated like shit. Correct?"

"Um. Yes, boss."

"You said as a child you were short, fat, and bullied. You told me the one thing you wanted most was respect."

"It's true."

I offered to pour him yet another shot, which he accepted.

"Then respect me by sharing the rest of your narrative. Start with the UNF. You claimed they sent you home because of myostemic plastosis. Your condition prohibited you from space travel, but the UNF has terrestrial facilities on every planet. You could've been assigned land duty. Not glamorous but ..."

Elian shaded his eyes beneath a hand.

"OK. Yes, boss. You're right. I failed the psych profile before they found the myostemia."

"Why?"

"I had a criminal record. Little dustups, mostly. Raul, I was different back then. I was angry. Like, all the time. I couldn't take their questions and those tests ... it wasn't fair."

He dropped his hand and rejoined his eyes to mine.

"All I wanted to do was go to space. I knew I'd be a better man if I left this damn planet."

"In my experience, running away introduces a new set of problems. So, Elian, your record and your emotional issues turned off potential employers. Yes?"

"The threats didn't help."

"Oh?"

"The first few times I received a vid dismissal, I sent them these long letters about how they'd regret not hiring me someday. I told

65

them I'd change the world and leave them behind. Once, I tried to force my way in to see an executive and ... I was arrested, of course. The rest of the industry blacklisted me."

"How old were you?"

"Nineteen."

"What happened next?"

"My parents threw me out. I tried to make do but ..."

"Life on the street poses many challenges. Yes?" He nodded. "I would know, Elian. I lived in the sewers of a city when I was sixteen."

The empathetic connection straightened him up.

"You, Raul?"

"Survival was a great teacher. Like you, I went by a different name. Ryllen. What is your true name, Elian?"

"Marcus Gallego."

Desperido had an unwritten rule: The "names before" were off-limits. Other than with Lumen and her son, I did not violate that tradition until today.

"Thank you and goodbye, Marcus. Now, back to present company. I killed a man when I was seventeen, the first of many. When did you begin, Elian?"

He exhaled a load that I suspected had been gathering for years.

"At first, it wasn't intentional. I got into a fight over ... shit, I don't even remember what. There was broken glass. I slashed the guy ... caught him in the neck. Thought I was done for, but I got shielded from arrest. A cartel."

"Horax?"

"No. The Monteros. They're based out of Inilqualit."

"Other side of the planet. Interesting."

"I did whatever work they assigned. For a while, I was a chemist. But there was trouble with a rival. The lab was bombed. The Monteros changed their tactics and gave me a new assignment."

I nodded with certainty.

"To kill."

"Among other things. I did those jobs for a year. I hated it, but I was good at it. Real good."

"Perhaps too good?"

My lieutenant leaned forward as if relieved of one hell of a weight.

"When they tried to take me out, I ran. I don't remember how I ended up in Machado and heard stories about Desperido. All I know is that living in a town where nobody wanted to be found was the best thing for me. After about a year, I stopped feeling afraid. That's my story, Raul. You're the only one here who knows."

I returned my pistol to the holster. Elian's eyes followed my hand until it closed my jacket to hide the weapon.

"I'm honored to be the first, my friend. You will never have to tell that story again."

"I want you to trust me, boss. I'll never let you down."

"That, I believe. You were a broken man, Elian. You found your way back without losing your mind or the talents you were taught. You're stronger with a true sense of self. I don't want my lieutenants to be mindless lackeys. I want men who share my vision and will murder anyone who stands between them and that vision.

"In the business we're embarking upon, compromise is a filthy word, second only to cowardice. We will take. Others will surrender. A simple path. In you, I need the genius who formulated Motif and the assassin who so impressed the Monteros that they tried to kill him. Elian, can I count on you to be both men?"

He jumped out of the copilot's seat and came around to me. Elian extended his hand.

"For life."

I couldn't guarantee he'd have much more of one, but I received his hand with a firm grip. Amazing how men responded when set free from the corner.

"For life, it is. Take your seat. I have a surprise."

Elian was too relieved to be alive to appreciate my next gift.

"Elian, I like your style, the black eye notwithstanding. I'm sure you don't miss the implant behind your ear."

"No, boss. Not at all."

"It's time to test the proposition."

I opened the worm drive tools and flipped the holo toward Elian.

"Select the charts and pick your destination."

Reality hit him. We were going up. My laser didn't kill him, but space might — if the drug Ripthenol hadn't actually cured his myostemia.

"We're doing this for real?"

"A dream fulfilled, my friend. Frightened?"

"Stunned. I kept my expectations low."

"Smart. I will warn you — the initial jump is challenging. You might think Bart is about to rip in half, but the journey will smooth out beyond the aperture. Why don't we start with something simple?" I pointed toward the Galactic Plane Navigational Model. "Let's stay in the neighborhood. Choose our current location. Good. Now, select a destination ten thousand kay beyond Frida's orbit."

He stabbed at the charts like he was afraid to break something.

"How about here, boss?"

"Good. Select it and allow the program to map the course. It will scan for potential obstacles." After he complied, the Nav outlined the coordinates. "All clear. Only 12.2 seconds. A short trip."

"Wow. That's it? I thought this tech would be more complicated."

"It's our greatest advance in flight. But yes, a six-year-old with curious fingers could cause havoc. Why do you think worm travel is so heavily regulated?"

"Where's the reporting function? There's no compliant transponder."

I snapped my fingers as if I'd overlooked something important.

"Oh. Damn. We forgot to install one with the other mods. Sad, isn't it? Guess we'll have to fly unobserved. Do you mind?"

He broke into a giddy fit.

"This is sweet, Raul. You're amazing."

"Yes. I am. So is the galaxy. Time to go see a bit of it." I pointed to the worm drive catalyzer. "Punch it. Then make yourself comfortable and enjoy the light show."

I knew what to expect, of course, and the brilliant flash that preceded the vortex felt routine. It transfixed Elian. I remembered my first sojourn into space. I was a soldier then, with the enemy staring from every direction. There weren't many 'firsts' anymore. After two thousand years, I'd given up on ever saying, "Now I've seen it all."

Bart buckled wildly, as he was wont to do entering the aperture, but I monitored his systems, which stabilized inside the wormhole's gray medium.

"I've seen vids," Elian said. "But there's nothing like the real thing. It's …" He choked up, just in time for us to exit the aperture.

I rotated Bart for the best viewing. Azteca sat in the center of the forward viewport, four hundred thousand kilometers distant. Strange old rock. As brown as it was green. The oceans were tiny. The cloud cover sparse. Somehow, it sustained a billion and a half people. Never understood why its moon Frida, which was water heavy and far less bleak, never caught on as an alternative.

Oh, well. The moment wasn't mine.

Elian's tears spoke for him.

"If the myostemia killed me, at least I'd die happy."

"Was it worth the wait?"

"More than. I'll never grow tired of it, Raul."

I adjusted Bart's attitude until Frida swung into view.

"Think of it, Elian. At this moment, there are 1.7 billion people on those two celestial bodies, and the vast majority will remain on the ground their entire lives. How many dream of being right where you are now, my friend?"

"Everyone."

"But most don't have the resources, the luck, or the drive to realize their dream. They'll die unfulfilled, Elian. Most humans do."

69

He wiped away his tears and sniffled a few times.

"Not me. I want to see it all, boss."

"That's my hope. You can become like a king. Your name known across dozens of systems. And like any king, you'll be loved and reviled. Elian, the bringer of Motif. Elian, the bringer of chaos and death. And when you're gone, you won't be forgotten. History finds a way to immortalize those who made a difference, for good or ill."

Mostly true. The People's Collectorate had gone to great lengths to pretend Moon and I didn't shape the current reality. As far as the official record was concerned, we died long ago in a fiery blaze above the planet Hokkaido.

Someday, they'd regret stuffing us away into a few ultra-classified files at Special Intelligence.

Eh. One step at a time.

I gave Elian as long as he needed to absorb the visual wonders. Then I took control of the worm drive and considered a new course.

Moon and I had heard nothing from 40-Cignus, which was neither positive nor unsettling. I didn't expect another job to come so soon after Qasi Ransome, but I also hadn't ruled out the possibility of a trap. Whoever destroyed the fort – the President's people or those reporting to Q6 – knew we weren't dead.

Bart had detected no irregular traffic in the Azteca system. If they were searching for us, these bastards were either discreet or chasing their asses on other planets. I felt drawn to that special asteroid.

Yet I reconsidered a jaunt to Cignus-40 when I remembered it was seventy minutes each way. My plates were still spinning in Desperido, and Lumen had scheduled a mid-afternoon wake for Hortense and Olive. Best we not return late.

A conspicuous absence now might shake the foundation I built with such care.

"Are you ready?" I asked.

"Sure. How long before the next trip, boss?"

"Uncertain, but I doubt your patience will run thin."

"One question. You've been traveling the stars for years. Do you ever get tired of sights like this?"

I avoided the honest answer.

"Some say the human race is living a miracle. Forty habitable worlds within nine hundred light-years of each other. The odds of that alone are infinitesimal. Elian, I don't find what I see on those planets to be of great interest. Humans are more or less the same wherever one journeys. The natural universe is where the beauty lies. So no, I never tire of these views."

"I won't either, boss. I can't thank you enough for this."

"You can start by promising not to tell. I'd rather not disclose Bart's full ability just yet."

"Understood. We went out for a training run. Routine."

And that's precisely how I wanted the rest of my day to proceed.

Naturally, I set expectations too high. After we completed a smooth landing and exited Bart, I saw a crowd gathering outside the cantina. Judging from the small group with fingers pointed, their presence had nothing to do with the scheduled wake.

We approached the locals, who were removing shards of glass. One of the tiny windows was busted.

"Tell me, Harlan, what happened?"

The thick-gutted artist who belonged to the militia leaned in and lowered his voice.

"She's lost her mind."

"Who?"

"Lumen."

"What happened?"

"Don't know. She ran out of her office in a rage and threw a tablet. I reckon she weren't trying, but she nailed that window. Bullseye. Never seen her like that before. Not even since you and Ilan took over the operation."

I suppose one peaceful, civilized day in the life of Desperido wasn't possible?

9

FROM DAY ONE, I CREDITED LUMEN with running a clean, orderly business. The cantina was well-apportioned (ridiculously so for a town of moles) and of the highest sanitary standards. Except for those times when disfigured and/or dead bodies created a mess. Mea culpa. So, I was unnerved to discover a disarray of Lumen's design.

In addition to the broken window, she hurled chairs into a booth. One lost a leg in the process. A handful of patrons nursed their beverages in the far corner, their fearful eyes directed toward the bar, where Lumen sat on a stool pouring from a tall bottle of green liquor.

She slouched.

Huh. That was new.

I'd expect it of a miserable drunk with nowhere else to hide.

Not this woman. Interesting.

I motioned for the patrons to vacate. They complied.

Yet on the way out, they stared at Lumen as if she were a stranger who wandered in from the desert rather than the woman who unified this town for three decades.

When we had the cantina to ourselves, I took up a spot several stools from Lumen, her tablet tucked in my jacket.

"So, I gather the wake has been postponed?"

"Ah, you fuc …" She gripped the bottle's neck like she wanted to fling it. "Don't start in on me, Raul. You're to blame for all of it."

"Oh, yes. That old saw. After two weeks, it's becoming tiresome. Very well. I'm responsible for the unraveling of your little desert empire. I take credit and blame in equal measure."

"And never once, an apology."

"In my experience, apologies are shallow. Since I wouldn't mean it, why should I?"

My honesty tied her tongue into a veritable knot.

"Lumen, we should focus on the matter at hand. You lost control. Something of great importance struck at your very core."

She finished a shot and wound the glass between her fingers.

"Before you and Ilan cursed my town, I hid a rifle behind the bar. No one knew about it – not even Ship. It was a last resort. The day you laid out those shot glasses in front of me, I almost reached."

I suspected as much.

"What stopped you?"

"Your partner."

"He would've killed you and everyone in the vicinity."

"You're evil, Raul. But Ilan? He's dangerous like no man I've met."

I softened my response with an ironic smile, but I doubt it helped.

"My partner's enemies tend to have short life spans. True. But a man of such caliber can be a magnificent ally. Now, what do you say we discuss your latest episode?"

"Some things can't be mended, even by a silver-tongued demon."

If only she knew …

In time. Perhaps.

"A women of your spinal fortitude does not collapse before many foes. My instinct points to two possible culprits: The past or the Children of Orpheus. There are gaps in your story, secrets you won't divulge. One of them snuck in through the back door."

"Why would I confess anything to *you*?"

"I'm an excellent listener." Not really, but I indulged humans so long as they got to the damn point. "Alternatively, I could call for Vash. He's out with Ilan and Ship plotting our upcoming maneuvers, but he might be better served here."

She jumped off her stool.

"Absolutely not. Leave him out of it."

"Ah. I see. Your son is the problem."

"You know nothing of this, Raul." She swept past me. "Leave it alone. Find Oren. He's a glass blower. He'll be able to fix the window. The wake is in one hour. I have to prepare."

She disappeared into her office; naturally, I followed.

"There will be no wake without a spot of truth-telling, Lumen."

"Get out."

"Your actions have unsettled your patrons. And your patrons are my contractors. Now, I can mitigate the incident with a clever falsehood. But I'll do no such thing until I examine the truth."

"Impossible bastard."

"In the flesh." More or less. "You hurled this tablet through a window. Any idiot could deduce you saw something on here that broke you. Unfortunately, the compeller slot is shattered, or I'd have taken a peek. When I complete the repair, I will. Let's save time, Lumen."

She kept a tidy office. A classic example of a place for everything, and for everything a place. Through one door, the kiosk and the supply cabinets. Through the other, her living space. I never ventured into either. I focused solely on the hub of Desperido: Lumen's desk and monitors which relayed data from the secure cams, the energy input from the sun globe, water levels in the cisterns, and all traffic through the town's single comms tower.

"It will change nothing, Raul."

"I disagree. Whatever you saw on the tablet is recorded on the tower's data spools. Who contacted you?"

"Guess, Raul. A man of your prodigious intellect should ..."

75

"Evelyn Cardinale." Her eyes confirmed it. "So, we received her response to last night's message."

"Yes." She laughed with a bizarre what-did-you-expect chuckle.

"I assume she's irritated. People hate when their accountants move on. It's quite a disruption."

"One day, Raul, that smirk will ..." She caught herself. Lumen knew insults and threats bounced off me. "Ask your question."

"May I see the transmission, please?"

She tapped the onscreen selections and expanded the offending vid. Then Lumen excused herself from the office without a word. I took a seat and pondered the monitor.

The woman who graced the screen appeared older and less regal than the grand senora about town I'd seen in my stream research. She wasn't draped in bejeweled excess, and she wore a simple house dress — far from the queen-of-the-day evening gowns worn at her many so-called philanthropic endeavors.

Stripped of her makeup and other accoutrements, the leader of the most feared cartel in the region resembled a tired woman of seventy, ten years older than her birth stamp.

Strange that a woman of such station would show her true haggard self for potentially public consumption. Unless, of course, she never expected it to be seen by anyone other than Lumen.

I played it.

"Hello, Yesenia. It's been too long."

Cardinale sat at a desk in an office overlooking gardens that transitioned to orchards stretching toward the horizon.

"I'd wish you good day and good health, if I thought you cared. To my everlasting chagrin, you made clear you don't."

She pretended to convey regret, but I heard the underlying tone. Nah, Senora Cardinale knew better than to raise her voice. She understood what all the longest-ruling assholes of history knew: Anger blinds.

"I have fond memories of my childhood. Remember all those

secrets we shared? The promises we made? Ah. We were so innocent in those days."

She paused for a spot of tea because, well, that's what proper women did. I reckoned. Especially the ones about to make ugly threats.

"So many mistakes. I've often regretted what happened during the reprisals, but never my efforts to save you from Papa. Never, that is, until now.

"Yesenia, I don't understand what changed. Why would you betray an arrangement that worked to everyone's benefit? Why tear asunder the only protection afforded your family?

"If you were unhappy with the terms of our deal, I would have lent an ear. Most contracts are amended over time. It's a necessity of business. But to return ten of my loyal Horax in a condition unfit for an open casket?"

Cardinale stared at the cam, fake grief oozing through her tight wrinkles. She paused for dramatic effect and cupped a hand over her mouth. Nice touch.

"I wish our families had never been parted. I wish you had stood at my side when I married Angel. I wish you had celebrated Ricardo and Amelia. Of all their aunts, they would have loved you best. Tia Yesenia. What a beautiful life it might have been.

"And now? What choice do I have? You broke our covenant. Mateo knows nothing of your son. When I tell him the truth, he'll rage at me for my decades of deception. He might even use it against me to shore up support for his ventures. But in the short term, his eye will be set upon your son.

"Yesenia, I do realize you have resourceful partners. Perhaps they misled you, or they never realized what you stood to lose. In that regard, what's soon to happen will be an avoidable tragedy. There is nothing you can say, no compensation fit for my losses. My sympathy for your plight is as dry as that wretched desert you call home.

"As I see it, you have one possible avenue of escape, though it is narrow. Send your son to Mateo. Allow him to beg forgiveness on your behalf. He will take the family name and cut all ties to the Rodriguez clan. Assuming, of course, Mateo chooses to keep him.

"You have two days. If he does not present himself at the gates of Hosta Grande Cardinale by sunset on the seventeenth, open caskets will be the least of anyone's concerns.

"I had such hopes for you and Desperido. But time lays wastes to all hope. It's our sad reality."

The vid ended.

As a god, I was used to making my own luck. Yet I enjoyed having it fall into my lap from unexpected directions. This particular intel filled in such a critical gap in my research, I was surprised Lumen didn't scrape it from the system.

I found her in the cantina trying to reattach a broken chair leg to no avail. I parked myself at the nearest table.

"Senora Cardinale intends to take more than her share of flesh. I assume you have no intention of turning over Vash."

She threw the broken leg aside.

"Evelyn will come for me regardless. There's nowhere on this planet I can hide."

"True. She does strike me as a relentless cunt. Let's deal with one issue at a time. Vash is the first-born son of the senior heir to the Cardinale fortune. That's quite a quandary."

"What a brilliant deduction, Raul."

"Does he know?"

She joined me at the table but did not sit.

"His father died before he was born. That's the only truth Vash will ever need."

"What if he were to show up at those gates and announce his true identity?"

"He'll be shot on sight. Evelyn will make sure. She won't risk the consequences."

"Which would be?"

"She and Mateo share the business. He's more of a functionary. He keeps their contacts in government and the constabulary aligned. But he's always resented the lack of full control."

"He's the eldest. What prevents him from taking it?"

"Mateo made the mistake of falling in love with a Rodriguez at the worst possible time. It was right after the Chancellors fell. Everyone was scrambling for power. Chancellor loyalists were being held to account. My family was ..."

"Defamed as loyalists even though they weren't."

She nodded. "I realized I was pregnant soon after our relationship was discovered. Mateo's parents forbid him from seeing me. The Cardinales were carefully arranging my family's destruction. Mateo towed the line, but Evelyn did not. I confided in her. She spoke on my behalf but never told them about the baby."

"I see. She removed you from the line of fire."

Lumen sighed. "I spent years at the parish of Todos Santos. After the reprisals ended and the Rodriguezes were no longer considered a threat, Evelyn arranged for me to travel here. Our deal was simple: My son never learned his lineage, I operated this town, and the Horax received a small tribute. She wanted to make Desperido look like a small business investment."

"And a safe haven for her people when they needed to be hid. Huh. She didn't know about your connections to the Children of Orpheus."

"No. My family guarded that allegiance to their graves."

"How did Mateo not inherit control?"

"Evelyn saw to it. She refused to play along as Mateo's subordinate, so she poisoned her father by exaggerating Mateo's affair with me and his supposed sympathy toward my family. The old man lost faith in his son and handed the fortune to Evelyn. After their parents passed, she projected herself as a benefactor."

"Impressive. She gave Mateo enough power to mollify his jealousy."

"Now he has a large family. Nine children, last I heard. Twenty grandchildren. Evelyn, on the other hand, has two children and was widowed, three times over. Her position is delicate."

I leaned back and took stock of this grand family melodrama. Thankfully, my own adoptive parents cast me out when I was sixteen. They assured I'd have no allegiance to anyone but myself.

This particular moment, however, reminded me of a simple tenet: For most humans, family still carried great value. It was both a strength and a crutch. I chose my next words carefully.

"Evelyn is the only Cardinale who knows about Vash. Correct?"

"Yes. If word had gotten back to Mateo, he would've scoured the planet for his son."

"That threat has governed your life for thirty-eight years."

"It has."

"And if that threat were eliminated ..."

She scrunched her hands into fists.

"What are you saying, Raul?"

"Nothing and everything, Lumen. I'm as good at fixing problems as I am creating them. And to be fair, I do owe you compensation for the mischief I brought to Desperido."

"You're a clever man, Raul. But what you propose is beyond your reach. She is untouchable."

"That's what she tells herself every day. She'll never see me coming. No one does."

I meant it literally, of course.

"Raul, are you trying to make a deal?"

"I am."

"What's your price?"

"The same thing I demand of all my business partners. Loyalty and transparency."

"A partner. For ...?"

"You'll decide, Lumen. If I free you of this burden, silence your antagonism. Support these things I intend to accomplish."

She leaned forward.

"And? As if I didn't already know."

"Full disclosure on Children of Orpheus. I want to know all their secrets. What are they planning to build and why?"

"What would you do with the knowledge? Create more mischief?"

"If I find it lucrative, I'll contribute. If not, I'll leave its future to the true believers. A smart businessman never leaves opportunity on the table. Yes?"

Lumen's eyes diverted toward the door. I glanced behind to see a few curious faces peek inside.

"They're here for the wake, Lumen. In the spirit of community healing, drinks on me. Take the afternoon and consider my proposal."

"You're mad."

"Sometimes. Yes. But not today."

I pushed out my chair and reached for the flask inside my jacket.

"Oh, and Lumen: A piece of advice. Stop throwing things. You frighten the patrons."

I left her to mull the only viable way out of her pickle and greeted the townsfolk at the door. They immediately inquired about Lumen.

"Fear not. She's fine, my friends. The grief of losing Hortense and Olive caught up with her today. Lumen needed to vent."

"Safe to go inside, is it?" Harlan asked.

"Lumen thinks of herself as the town's mother. She takes the loss of her children seriously. It's good she cares. Agree?"

"Tell the truth, Raul, she never showed an inclination before now."

That might've explained why my takeover met little resistance. I imparted a dose of dubious psychology.

"We humans are two-faced. We present one exterior to administer our daily lives, while we conceal our true selves for fear the world will not understand us. Lumen has a huge heart, but she wants no one to mistake it for weakness, so she hides it. Today, her heart briefly took control. She responded with rage. I assure you, she's fine now."

81

They accepted my analysis with shrugs, sighs of relief, and – dare I say it – softened expressions that suggested empathy. My dulcet tone assuaged their anxiety, which led me to a simple conclusion:

People respected Raul Torreta the man as much as the salesman. That I was also a killer seemed unimportant.

My charm soothed the restless souls of the unwashed masses.

That was not, however, the approach I took minutes later when I hooked up with Moon, Ship, and Vash. They returned from the southern defense perimeter.

"Where do we stand?"

Moon and Vash shared an uneasy glance, but they nodded in unison. Was it possible they'd spent the past two hours having an actual grown-up dialogue free of personal animosity?

"We finalized details for the home defense," Moon said.

Vash agreed. "This town will be buttoned up. They can hit us on two fronts. We've got the goods to shut them down."

I turned to Ship. "Learn anything today, kid?"

The boy shuffled his feet in the red dust.

"It's gonna be nasty, boss. I reckon we won't all make it out."

"There will be casualties. No war is won without a body count."

Ship's hat shaded his eyes, but they glowed with a fire I hadn't seen in the boy.

"I want a bigger role, boss. I'm your lieutenant. I should be on the tumbler with you."

Vash and Moon, standing behind the kid, shook their heads. Apparently, last night's debacle in the cantina left them unconvinced Ship could handle himself amid the firing line.

"We'll discuss it later. The wake will be starting soon. Lumen could use your help."

Ship walked away sulking. Poor kid: Right when he thought he'd graduated from humble server to assassin's apprentice.

I thanked Vash for his help and waited until he left me alone with my partner.

"I bring fun news, my friend. Two fronts won't finish the job. The new and glorious Army of Desperido will fight on three."

Moon's eyes twinkled.

10

A PROPER ASSASSIN EXCELLED if he followed a simple rule: Ignore grief. Never fall for a widow's tears or a child's wails. An assassin doomed his career when he allowed the first hint of remorse or sympathy into his conscience. When I was a teenager, I started my portfolio as a terrorist. The group claimed each murder elevated the cause. Thus, I learned how to look away; the consequences never mattered.

That technique proved more challenging at the wake for Olive and Hortense, a pair of women I didn't know but whose deaths had shaken the town and undermined my efforts.

I meandered through the crowd, which filled the cantina to standing room. Half of Desperido showed within the first half hour, although many came for the free libation. I heard a disconcerting mix of rumors about the murder scene to random name-dropping of potential suspects. Most locals assumed a competitor took out the women, but few knew anything about their product line. They tried to comfort themselves with the theory that this was a one-time, targeted hit, not the opening stanza of a serial killer.

Or the psychotic murder porn of a fallen serpent god.

I didn't walk ten feet without being asked to espouse my own theory or if I expected to solve the crime soon. After the first improvisations, I developed a common response.

"The investigation is proceeding. We should have a resolution very soon. You need not worry. Our town is safe and prosperous."

They treated me with the respect of constable *and* mayor, titles which I found exhilarating. However, those unofficial designations did not serve me well when I happened upon a few who allowed their shock and fear to generate tears.

I was a wolf god, not a grief counselor.

"Knew Olive on and off for six years," said Marley, who was in talks with Elian to integrate Motif wafers into the linings of her cosmetic products. "She was a troubled woman when she pulled into town, Raul. Much like most of us, she had a story worth forgetting." The fortysomething woman with ginger-dyed hair blew her nose into a handkerchief.

"But Olive ... she worked hard to make friends. That don't go over easy in Desperido. We hold to a cynical disposition. Until you come along, Raul. At any rate, I took fondly to Olive. We had many pleasant encounters.

"Couple years back, I moved over to House 37, and we lost some of that connection. But she confided in me about three months ago. She and Hortense thought they were in love. The light was fully restored. And now this. Both, Raul. *Both!*"

The story produced a few tears from those who listened. Heads bowed from people who probably never said two words to the alleged lovers. Though the intel provided an insight I did not learn from their roommate Ev, the mere presence of a romance appeared to strike a chord. These folks hid themselves from the world like rabbits in burrows, usually choosing to find their sexual solace in care workers rather than meaningful relationships. For one to rise in our little desert refuge only added to the melancholy.

I searched for a political response because emotional solace was not my flavor.

"This was an unspeakable tragedy, my friends. When true love is cut short, it impacts everyone who was witness to its beauty. We should learn from what we lost and embrace every moment we have together. Profit margins are important, of course, but life has to be about so much more. It's about the relationships. Yes?"

On balance, I thought my answer went over well, although smiles were scarce and tears too frequent for my taste.

Others shared their reminiscences about the departed, some with me, others at a designated opportunity for anyone to speak to the full crowd. Their words varied between maudlin, reflective, and incoherent. These people dealt with death about as well as I did.

The guilty party stood outside the cantina, ostensibly to remain on alert for potential Horax reprisals. Moon wanted no part of this business. He preferred to smoke his cigar in peace and contemplate the details about our upcoming fight on three fronts. My news, which guaranteed a heightened potential for bloodshed, excited him.

In exchange for that joy, I insisted he follow certain terms. The first: Do not kill our contractors.

"You placed us in a dangerous position," I warned my partner before the wake began. "This town's confidence in our leadership will collapse if we don't contain the problem. They'll demand swift resolution, and it must be clean, with no further threat to their lives."

"Would that be so awful? If there's an uprising, we'll slip into Bart and be off-world in minutes. We can go anywhere, and they don't know our true form."

"These people will be slaughtered."

"You act like you care."

"We're building an enterprise. People have placed their trust in us."

"*You.* No one trusts me, Royal."

He said it without a hint of resentment.

"But they'll work with you to serve a common interest. Hell, even Vash put up with your funereal attitude. Moon, when we've done all we can to lay the groundwork on Azteca, we'll expand our operation.

In the meantime, cool your syneth and only slaughter Horax."

Moon grunted his assent, but I trusted him only slightly more than our mortal acolytes. However, that conversation told me what must be done today to keep this town under my thumb until the tumbler arrived in two days. I visited the scene of the crime long enough to secure the objects I required and joined the wake.

My mission began by pulling Ev aside. She was exhausted – perhaps by the stares and whispers more than any semblance of grief. Of course, she was a suspect in many eyes. No doubt, some folks suspected her of staging the "discovery" of the bodies to throw everyone off the trail. She had risen to the top of my suspect list before I opened my eyes to the truth.

"How are you holding up, my friend?"

Ev stayed close to the bar and drank liquor like water.

"Never shoulda come, boss. They all reckon I done it."

I set her half-empty glass on the bar. We faced the crowd, though Ev avoided direct eye contact.

"Not true, Ev. People reach for the laziest conclusions when they lack anything tangible to hold onto."

"Eh. No." She slurred her speech looking for an answer. "They're thinking ol' Ev done lost her mind."

"That's the whiskey talking. Tell me something, Ev. Did you get some sleep in the new house?"

"Laid on the cot. Closed muh eyes. Done saw nothing but blood pouring out their necks and ..."

I wrapped my arm around her and held tight. The poor woman needed to feel safe. Despite scant experience comforting anyone – human or otherwise – I was a visual learner, and these techniques seemed to work on most folks.

This wasn't my preferred course, but the town wanted resolution. It needed to put a face on the killer.

"Sleep is your best remedy." I reached into my pocket. "A long, fruitful sleep refreshes the mind and brings perspective. You'll approach the day with renewed optimism."

I dropped a small tablet into her liquor. It dissolved at once.

"Here." I handed her the glass. "Finish and go home. I don't want to hear from you until tomorrow. You'll feel better, Ev. Trust me."

"What about my products? They ain't ready for inventory."

"Skip a week, my friend. If you're running low on credits, I'll cover your debt."

Ev stared into the last of that golden liquid. For a moment, I thought she wouldn't drink.

"That's might friendly, Raul. But I ... I want to carry my weight."

"You will. Next week."

"If the town ain't run me off by then."

"No worries, Ev. I expect to resolve the case later today. You'll be thoroughly exonerated."

That nudge pumped her with just enough energy to throw back the rest of her drink and stare up at me with a crooked smile.

"Life sure took a turn when you done come along, Raul."

That had been pretty much a common refrain all my lives.

Ryllen. Royal. Raul. Names not starting with R.

"I'm what you call a disruptor; I shake people out of their routine. You see, Ev, life is meant to be lived, not endured. Starting tomorrow, this nasty business will be in the rearview and you'll charge forward."

Ev squeezed me tight before straightening herself out and pushing through the gathered masses. I thought about escorting her home to ensure she made it before the tablet kicked in. But that would have raised too many damn questions.

I returned to my role as man of the people. For the next hour, I listened to their banter. The funereal atmosphere disappeared as they imbibed and perhaps even forgot the original purpose of this gathering. My bank account took a considerable hit as bottle after bottle emptied. A minor inconvenience to solve a larger problem.

Vash had pitched in to help his mother and Ship handle the burden from behind the bar. I waited for a moment when Lumen was not refilling glasses to pull her aside.

"You're not much for speeches, but now seems an opportune time. They're well and truly sloshed, and the wake has served its purpose. Say a few words, and I'll handle the heavy lifting."

Lumen had no leverage to refuse. She called over her son and Ship to pass along the news. Then she displayed a talent heretofore unknown: She placed a finger in each corner of her mouth and let loose a piercing whistle which overwhelmed the sea of voices.

She waited until she had their full attention — as in, time to shut the hell up and pay attention.

"I'll keep it brief," she shouted. "Thank you for turning out. Hortense and Olive would be happy to know you cared. Truth is, you're pissing away my stock. The day's not done, and tomorrow your products need to be ready when we take inventory. Some of you'd be best served heading back home and finishing work."

They weren't uplifting words, but I reckoned Lumen wasn't in the mood for uplifting — assuming she knew how to fake it.

"I'd appreciate if you dropped you off the glasses at the bar on the way out. Sure would make life easier."

She nodded my way. "Anything to add, Raul?"

"Unfortunately, I do."

Before my little game reached its dramatic climax, I made a mental diversion.

"Theo?"

He grumbled, of course. *"Yeah. Whatcha want, old man?"*

"Speak to Addis. Have her convince Moon to come inside at once. He needs to see this."

"Heh! I know whatcha done to that woman. It might impress the home folks, but you're only biding time before Moon strikes again."

"Yes, Theo. I am. It's called strategy. Take one problem off the board to focus on the next. Speak to Addis. Now."

"Cool your syneth. I'm on it."

I hoped Moon wasn't so stubborn he'd ignore his *D'ru-shaya*. He needed to see me resolve the mess he created.

"First, I want to thank Lumen for showing true leadership at a time of shock and grief. She has put herself on the line for this town going on three decades. Please share your appreciation."

Yeah, it was a stalling tactic but one that worked. The applause started slowly – with my assistance – and grew to a rousing crescendo. I doubted these people appreciated Lumen like they should have, but the liquor opened their hearts.

"Now, as Lumen said, we will conduct inventory tomorrow. I intend to begin the process by nine. Your tallies must be finalized and accurate. We're two days from the largest, most lucrative distribution in the history of Desperido. At stake is nothing less than the future of this community. To that end, I want you to enter this next phase secure in the notion that you are safe and protected."

The cantina door opened with a creak. Moon didn't expect to draw so many eyes. He stepped inside and leaned against the wall.

"Ilan and I have invested in you. Consequently, everything we do is in your service. With the help of Lumen and her son, we began an immediate investigation into the double murders. A few hours ago, we solved the case."

I waited for the murmurs to settle before continuing. Moon crossed his arms. Did he have an idea how I intended to undercut his plans?

"The evidence was clear. We acquired the murder weapon, which included fingerprints and genetic stamps in the dried blood. All that remained was securing a confession. I did not want to come forward until there was no doubt.

"My friends, I must say I am conflicted. The individual who killed Hortense and Olive did so in a moment of passion. As some of you confided in me today, the victims were intimate. In love, so you said.

"Unfortunately, a third woman was involved, equally in love with Hortense, who rejected her in favor of Olive. The killer was unable to

90

accept the circumstance. However, in her confession, she told me of plans to leave Desperido rather than face rejection.

"Last night, as we prepared to defend the town against the Horax, this woman gave in to her jealousy. She confronted the victims, who rejected her again and demanded she move out in the morning."

The crowd's murmurs returned, their suspicions now confirmed.

"Yes, I speak of Evangeline. I interviewed her this morning. She was contrite, even devastated over her actions. She said it all happened so fast, she barely remembered it. Ev attended this wake at my insistence. I wanted her to face the reality of what she'd done. I knew she posed no threat to anyone else. She was a broken woman of limited means. I allowed her to leave on her own recognizance because she has nowhere to run.

"Her last words were: 'Whatever the punishment, make it quick. Please don't send me to the desert.' That judgment will fall on another day. My friends, I ask that we refrain from castigating this woman. She reached for something elusive – the love of another – and lost her mind in the face of rejection.

"How many of you came to Desperido because you were rejected? Thrown away? Forgotten?"

I doubted the equivocation would work for long. Barring a sudden demand for a good old-fashioned public hanging, this matter would soon end in peace.

"I'll be more than happy to answer your questions later. Until then, my friends, return to your homes. You are safe."

The momentum toward the single exit was slow and uncertain. The revelation comforted no one, which didn't shock me. These desert rats weren't much for community spirit, but murder by one of their own kind was unheard of (outsiders excluded, of course).

Moon revealed nary a hint of bother; though to be fair, he had mastered a stoical expression. In time, he joined the exodus in a cloud of cigar smoke.

Hundreds of empty glasses scattered on tables and the bar would require many loads through the sani-drone. Honesty, I didn't realize Lumen had such a large supply.

"I'll hang around to help as needed," I told Lumen while the crowd thinned. She shook her head.

"The cleanup don't bother me, Raul. I've been handling this town's messes for thirty years." She lowered her voice for me and Vash. "That story you told ... I don't believe it. Nor do you."

"I'm sorry, Lumen. The evidence is ..."

"Strong. Yes. Ev had the means and a motive. But about that knife. When did you find it?"

"As I said, Ilan and I worked hard to resolve the mystery. And now it is."

Vash interjected. "Did you record her confession?"

"It wasn't necessary. She won't hide from her guilt."

"What about the filamine poisoning? How does that ...?"

"Set aside your doubts, Vash. It's done. All that's left now is to determine Ev's sentence and how to dispose of the bodies. Both items should be finalized before the tumbler arrives."

They didn't trust me, and with good goddamn reason. They might pursue the dangling holes in my conclusion, but their efforts wouldn't be worth spit.

They'd never have a chance to question Evangeline.

No one would.

The thousand milligram dose of filamine had done its job by then.

11

S LEEP WASN'T MY GIG, so I watched many Aztecan sunrises. This one felt different. The sun's upper half consumed most of the desert horizon in a fleeting moment of fiery splendor. I adjusted my optical sensors to embrace the searing light.

Billions of humans drank café to start the day; I found my energy in the output of a white-hot star. What I also discovered with my heat-intensive breakfast was a twinge of something unfamiliar.

It started in my gut. Not exactly an upset stomach, given that the organ located there performed an unrelated function. I almost asked Theo to probe my syneth core for anomalies.

Then it came to me. A flash from too long ago.

I was a kid running around with a terrorist group called Green Sun. One night we were ambushed by an opposition force. The bastards wiped us out – myself included. Yep. Those assholes understood the thrill of a well-executed ambush. That was the first time I died.

When I woke, having mysteriously recovered from several kill shots, I walked past the bodies of my brothers and sisters and found my mentor, roommate, and lover. He was a bloody mess.

Ran fast as I could, trying to make sense of it all. Only later did I learn of my immortality. In the meantime, I would've preferred to have died with my comrades.

Regret.

It consumed me that night. Now, it rose in my belly as a nasty little reminder of my human heritage.

Had it been that long? Was there nothing in the past two thousand years I regretted until now?

I searched and came up dry.

Damn. Talk about living for the future!

What did I regret? Sentencing Ev to death for a crime she didn't commit? Betraying the woman's trust and fealty? Allowing three Desperidans to die because I was blind to Moon's discontent?

The bigger question worth answering:

Why did these things bother me at all?

I killed tens of thousands of humans and a species called Creators. I slaughtered them up close. Mine was the last face they saw before the final ember of their lives flickered to black. And me?

I moved on. Never looked back. Justified every corpse.

What changed?

Three forgotten nobodies in a town hardly worth the space on a map. Three broken humans. And now their deaths bothered me.

Shit.

"Whatcha think, Theo? Was Moon right? Was taking over this town a mistake?"

Sometimes, my *D'ru-shaya* made sounds to indicate impatience or even, gosh forbid, to signal he didn't want to be disturbed. This time, I heard the moan of a half-asleep man turning over in bed.

"Hold on, dumbass. Am I hearing you right? You want my advice?"

"Not your advice, Theo. I know better. A simple analysis."

"I'm many things, Royal, most of which you conveniently forgot. But I ain't a qualified therapist."

That brought a smile to my face.

"You've been the voice in my head for centuries. I believe you're

more than qualified to analyze me. Just ... leave out the name-calling. It's a tired old shtick."

"Heh. I'm not a creative mastermind like you, Royal. I resort to repetition and denigration. Old habits."

"Understood. You're ancient, underutilized, underappreciated, and sexually deprived. It's a shitty combination. How about answering my question, and we'll go from there. Should I regret ignoring Moon's concerns about taking over Desperido?"

Theo shifted his tone from the usual caustic demeanor to a smug, upper class look-down-the-nose approach.

"Royal, you never allowed anyone to shape your future. You exploited your teachers – especially my namesake. You fed off the skillsets of anyone in your orbit. Moon was the only one you ever considered your equal, and even he walks in your shadow. You parse gifts to keep him at bay. Why regret a winning strategy?"

"You're saying I'm a narcissist."

"Your word, not mine."

"But accurate?"

"Oh, yes. Most definitely."

Eh. Not a surprise. I mean, if you can't love yourself ...

"A narcissist won't change for anyone."

"True, Royal."

"So the takeover was a good idea. But the execution was ..."

"Bolloxed."

I searched my language bases but came up empty.

"Did you just make up a word, Theo?"

"Not at all. I collected it during our travels to the Quaternary Universe. Earth. Remember now?"

I hadn't thought to search for slang beyond our Alpha Universe.

"Bolloxed. Yes. That's a nice one. I should use it more often. So, Theo, in your analysis, what did I bollox?"

"Many things were a close call, Royal. But you assumed everyone would follow your script. So many did that you easily overlooked the

95

wildcard in your midst. You knew Moon was volatile. He never fully recaptured his sanity. You knew these people were in danger the longer you remained. You assumed Moon wouldn't break out of his cage. Now, you're too close to these people. You claim they're your employees, but you think of them like children."

It was a fair, dispassionate, and unsurprising perspective – but for the last few words.

"Children? I think your analogy missed the mark, my friend."

"Nope. You brought them into the light. Showed them how to create stronger businesses, build community, and fight for their home. They aren't the mole people anymore. Who could do all that but a father?"

"OK. Fine. How about we agree on 'father figure'?"

"If that helps you, Royal."

"It does, Theo. So, as Desperido's father figure, I feel regret over having lost three of my sort-of children. Yes?"

"Not regret. Guilt. That's what you're feeling, Royal. One you killed, the other two you allowed to die because you weren't paying attention. All a product of your narcissism."

The full sun crested above the horizon. It seemed to have shrunk by half. Ah. Those fleeting moments of beauty …

"I have a final question, Theo."

"Yes?"

"Do you bill by the hour?"

"Hah. I'll be taking a piece out of you for eternity."

"I was afraid you'd say that. This has been helpful, Theo. An actual dialogue with honesty and sincerity. It's been civil and enlightening."

Theo went quiet. In fact, I couldn't detect the sonofabitch for a minute or so. Then he reemerged, laughing like a damn hyena.

"Don't get used to it, dumbass."

"Fool's gold, I reckon."

"And guess who's the fool, old man?"

I didn't wallow in Theo's verbal victory. If the moment gave my *D'ru-shaya* some comfort, who was I to be annoyed? Plus, he offered insight that ventured into a domain I thought impossible:

Guilt.

Three dead humans. One at my hands.

Guilt. A very close cousin to *remorse*, the mortal enemy of an upper-tier assassin.

I didn't know what to make of it. Or worse, what it meant as the bloodiest event of our occupation neared.

One certainty was clear: This particular virus did not infect my partner. Nor would it ever.

Moon returned to town on a rifter minutes later and straddled the vehicle alongside me.

"Done," he said with nary a hint of bother.

"This was the best way."

While the town slept, we gathered the three bodies and their belongings onto the rifter. Moon took them three kilometers south and incinerated the cargo. As a courtesy, I told Lumen what we intended, except I substituted 'burial.'

She agreed with a quick, quiet operation. Desperido was in too deep to allow this distraction to divert it from the next, potentially existential task. I saw it in her weary but resigned demeanor: She'd always blame me (rightfully, I suppose) for backing her into his corner, but she saw no option other than to play along.

Moon, on the other hand, enjoyed playing with fire. When I offered to assist in the disposal, he turned me away with a dismissive grunt.

"We're finished with these people after tomorrow," Moon said upon his return, not a hint of compromise in his tone. "Win on all three fronts, take our lieutenants and our profits, and leave Azteca."

"That's your mandate, my friend?"

"We'll draw too much attention, Royal. You always said the key to long-term success was to cook this plan on simmer. Now, you expect

97

us to blow up the world and think nobody will notice."

I tried not to sound condescending.

"We're going to kill mobsters and assassins, my friend. Their losses will not shake the establishment. Many are likely to cheer the news."

"News will make it back to the President and Q6. They'll see the patterns. The proximity to the Fort of Inarra won't be considered a consequence."

A valid point I'd already taken into account.

"They're hamstrung, Moon. They won't send in agents or ships to scour populated areas. Not even Desperido. Moreover, we have an agreement with the President to kill her enemies. I doubt she's done with us. Our bank account must grow."

"You're putting all our plans at risk."

I turned away from Moon and toward the town. It glowed like copper on fire.

"We've done this routine to death, my friend. I ain't gonna rehash why this strategy will build our future. You wouldn't by chance lack confidence in your own plan?"

As part of my co-leadership concession, I handed to Moon the defense of Desperido and our strategy against the inevitable Horax reprisals. Our success tomorrow hinged on his ability to communicate all parts of the plan to our willing participants.

"I left nothing out, partner. We'll leave winners."

"And this town subject to the fallout."

"These ruins were here centuries before we showed. They'll be here long after. Tenants will change, but that's mortals for you."

"No concern in the least for what we leave behind?"

He pushed on the rifter's nav arm.

"We're Destroyers, you and me. Where we go, people die. Forgot already, partner?"

Moon didn't wait for a reply. He zipped into town to park the rifter outside the supply depot with the others.

He never expressed his feelings after my public resolution to his double murder. Perhaps he predicted I'd find a way out of the conundrum before he pounced on another victim.

I'd have to confront him after we defeated the Horax and Cardinale, a proposition more fraught than anything we'd encounter on the tumbler. For now, I rested my hopes on one outcome:

Moon would see the totality of our victories and realize I was right about these Desperidans.

The alternative? Well, that would be a game-time decision.

Which is why, by and large, I stuck to business per usual that day. Along with Lumen and Ship and a hefty assist from Elian, I oversaw the inventory and entered the town's products into a pair of digital manifests: Legitimate and otherwise.

Our contractors arrived at the depot in orderly fashion over the course of five hours. Despite much harangue over the murders and a hefty consumption of liquor at the wake, my people did a bang-on job of arranging their products for distribution to buyers.

Silver case after case passed inspection. Profit projections exceeded last week by five hundred percent.

Smiles all around for the contractors with the largest gains, but few cheers. Many were exhausted bringing their wares to market on such a timeline. Considering the risk that tomorrow's tumbler might struggle to reach its many destinations, celebrations were at best muted. Yet everyone who entered a product line onto the initial inventory list delivered before close of business.

Nice.

As afternoon approached evening and the depot cleared of all but me and my new lieutenants, I took a moment to appreciate both. I couldn't have changed the equation so quickly without them.

Yes, even a narcissist can admit he doesn't do it all by himself.

I wrapped my arms around Elian and Ship as we studied the wall against which the bounty of Elian's team dominated.

"Take a good look, my friends. Think about where your lives were three weeks ago."

Ship laughed. "I had a claw and I talked with a fake accent."

"Funny thing is," Elian said, "nobody believed that was your real voice. The shit people said."

Amid a huge gulp, Ship replied: "Like what?"

"Jokes, mostly. They don't mean nothing now, kid."

I intervened before the boy wallowed in self-pity.

"It's true, Ship. You've earned respect. When people see you in the company of me or Ilan, they know you're a power player."

He couldn't hide that aw-shucks grin before pointing to the half million credits worth of Elian's products.

"I don't have much juice compared to Elian. I mean, look at all this." My lieutenants had put their brief spat into the past. Ship flicked his hand at Elian. "You're the one making the town look great."

"Hey, you'll get there, Ship. Ain't that right, boss?"

"Oh, sure. Ship's taking a different route to prosperity, but his name will shine alongside yours someday."

"First," the kid said, "I need to learn a real craft. I mean, I don't intend to compete with Elian's trade, but I could use a good teacher."

"Yeah, no. You've already started work on your craft, my friend. Elian will be the most feared drug lord in the forty worlds. He'll rule an empire his predecessors only dreamed of. Rich beyond measure. You, my friend, will be the main reason he'll be feared."

"How's that?"

"Because your craft will be to kill anyone who challenges that empire or mine. When people hear you're coming, they'll run for their lives."

Now that vision might have beefed up the ego of a typical wannabe or assassin's apprentice, but Ship didn't straighten his shoulders. I felt the uncertainty in his diminished stature.

"Those are big plans you got for me, boss, but I ain't even killed anybody yet. And I blew my first chance."

"Eh. Beginner's bad luck. I knew a fella once who was timid. Not much older than you. He couldn't bring himself to kill a man until he was cornered. Now, he's the fastest trigger in the universe."

"You, boss?"

I chuckled. "No. I was many things as a kid, but timid weren't among my qualities. I speak of Ilan."

Ship frowned, but I knew it came from a place of respect.

"I could never be like him."

"Then you'll be dead before your seventeenth birthday. Trust me, Ship. You'll get there. The road is long and curvaceous, but it's not without end. We'll have to put some beef on those muscles, of course, and I suspect you're in for a nice growth spurt. Whatcha think, Elian? Can the kid become our chief enforcer?"

Elian reached across with a balled fist, which Ship bumped.

"There's no dream too big with you guiding us, boss."

I loved the dulcet tone of those words.

Yep.

It was entirely possible one or both might meet their untimely demise tomorrow. However, every day was a gamble in this line of work. I wasn't worried about Elian in the short term. His role seemed relatively safe. But Ship?

Damned if the kid didn't weasel his way onto tumbler defense duty. He used the time with Vash and Moon to make his case.

Wasn't much I could do now but hope he didn't hesitate again.

I planned to be with him on the day he returned to Everdeen to take care of some longstanding family business.

Yep. Big dreams, indeed.

"My friends, what we have in this depot will earn the town more than four hundred thousand UCVs. And it's just a trickle to what awaits. You two ready to send a message the Horax won't forget?"

"Yes, boss," they said in unison.

"Sensational. Then whatcha say we head on over to the cantina for the final strategy session. Let's see if Ilan and Vash have cooked up any new surprises for our Horax friends."

"It's going to be a big day, boss," Ship said. "I'll be ready."

Famous last words.

12

MOON GOT TO THE POINT when addressing the three dozen of us in attendance: "Everyone has a post to defend. No one deviates unless you hear different from me, Raul, or Vash."

He laid out the defensive positions for holding the town, assuming the Horax sent in a rearguard action, as we anticipated. He had created a lovely holoplat of Desperido which laid out the grid, assigned locations, and simulated scenarios under which the Horax might attack.

He focused much of his time on Elian, who would be Bart's pilot and whose role would be dictated based on the nastiness of the local fight versus the battle on the northern road to Machado.

Elian would be the first human to control Bart's Nav since we bought that turquoise beauty. It was an unsettling thought, but I trusted Elian. He was a good listener who showed sufficient skill in his training flights. Plus, he had too much at stake: Blow the operation, and he stood to lose his Motif lab and/or his biggest shipment to date.

"The perimeter shield will keep out their vehicles unless they have the tech to adapt," Moon continued, emphasizing this point to the ground militia. "Assume they will."

He pointed to the mines which dotted the desert.

"These mines don't require physical contact. Each contains a five-meter proximity detector. The AI will analyze a target's course, wait until the target reaches its closest position to the mine, and detonate. Any human within two meters goes down straightaway. Beyond that, it depends on how much armor they wear."

He emphasized the need to delay firing on invaders who survived the minefield. Don't give up your sniper positions too soon. Vash's lieutenants, Oria and Den, would oversee that end of the operation.

A hand rose among the town's defenders.

"What if they come at us from the air?" Saul, an art forger, spoke for most. "Can't those bastards bomb us to death?"

"They can try," Moon said, "but the shield will scramble a missile's payload guidance. It won't detonate at impact."

Vash intervened.

"The Horax is a criminal organization, but it won't dare violate certain laws. The Collectorate Constitution restricts the use of aerial bombardment to the United Naval Forces and each government's domestic air force. And even then, they have to jump through hoops to receive authorization. Any outliers will be detected by the satdrone network. I've heard stories about what happens to people who try to skirt around the law. It's not pretty."

Huh. I knew about the law but didn't think of it the night a ship blew the Fort of Inarra into nonexistence without consequence. I doubted whoever pulled those strings faced any hoops.

The answers appeared to satisfy the ground defense team. If I didn't know any better, I'd say Moon and Vash worked well together. Not bad, considering Vash arrived in Desperido to kill us, and we took out his entire team in return.

"Now we'll review the tumbler defenses," Moon said before he deferred to Vash.

I enjoyed playing spectator. Nice change of pace.

Vash threw open a detailed holo of the six-section road train. Four cargo holds connected by a bridge system were bookended by identical navigation cabs. Fifty meters front to back. Ten sets of wheels taller than a man on either side.

Like with Moon's design, Vash designated where each of our team would be located.

"A few reminders. The tumblers are equipped with a crew of twelve. One navigator per cab. Crew quarters located here and here," he said, pointing to cargo holds one and four, adjacent to the cabs. "This is where you'll find them during transit. These quarters are compact, designed with six bunks, a kiosk, and a toilet.

"After the crew has stowed our inventory, they'll retreat to these quarters. That's two auditors, six loaders, and two alternates. Our goal: Keep them contained there until the Horax threat is eliminated. They won't know what we're up against, but some of them might be stupid enough to play Fast-Gun Jose."

Ship, who was to be stationed in cargo hold three, raised a hand.

"Do they have access to weapons other than their sidearms?"

"Officially, no. The Montez Shipping Group has strict guidelines. The crew are trained and licensed to carry Stahl Mark 9 pistols, but these are kept under lock in the crew quarters unless the tumbler is traveling through known agitator zones or off-loading in a high-crime port."

"You said *officially.*"

Others nodded. They picked up on how Vash hedged his bets.

"I worked on these trains for six years," Vash replied. "The navigators sometimes smuggle rifles onboard for difficult routes. They're paranoid. I haven't heard of a major hit on a train in ages. It's usually a minor disturbance. An amateur blockade. A strike-and-grab at a small depot.

"These guys are armed, but they are *not* fighters. Most are Montez employees, accountable to their guild. They don't go looking for trouble. The same can't be said for the independent agents, like those who handle Desperido's illicit trade for cargo hold three. Their number varies, anywhere from two to five. Montez has to employ a majority from the guild, but the others are hired at its discretion."

"Do you have the staff manifest for this particular train?" I asked.

"Yes, Raul. It came through an hour ago. Four indies, including the auditor. They pulled out of Ciudad Huzzanor three hours ago with a fresh crew. They'll be on Day 2 when they reach us. We're the nineteenth stop."

The crews worked three-day shifts and covered thousands of kilometers. There might have been faster ways to ship goods across this planet, but the road trains had operated for so long and efficiently under guild regulations, any push for change went nowhere. Vash didn't discuss how his group of assassins arranged transit on a tumbler weeks earlier, but I doubted he wanted any reminders of that debacle.

"Now, there will be consternation when our team boards," Vash continued. "Initially, we'll enter cargo three with our products. After the indies stow our cases, we'll fan out to our stations. That's ten men with rifles they are not expecting. If you encounter pushback, just say we're there under special contract to the Montez Group, and we'll disembark at the Machado North Province Depot. It's bullshit, but it will buy us time.

"Raul will make his way to the navigator. Once he takes control of the forward cab, we'll have the train. We'll seal the crew inside their quarters front and aft and prepare for the ambush."

Moon and Vash wisely agreed to position me at the front. No one was better suited to talk down the navigator from his inevitably agitated state.

Vash continued his explanation of the train's architecture. He noted access points between cargo holds, maintenance hatches down below and to the roof, and described the secure locking system for the sliding cargo doors.

Moon took over the presentation, pointing out the geography between Desperido and the Machado region. In the last few days, he sent out several "sighters" along Roadway 9, as it was officially known. These drones patched into our network and would give us a heads-up to enemy positions for the first seventy kilometers, the range where we expected the Horax to hit.

"It's possible they'll set up a blockade on the straightaway," he said, "but it wouldn't make sense. The navigator would have plenty of time to reverse course or go off-road, which the tumbler can do. We expect the most likely choke point to come here."

He pointed to a location in the first knolls of the Ogala Hills. Roadway 9 veered northeast at forty degrees.

"There's a blind spot four hundred meters long. There's no off-road escape. Most likely, they'll hide behind the scrub brush in that zone until the tumbler passes southbound. Then they'll set up and wait."

"So, if there's a blockade," said Saul, "what happens?"

Moon deferred to me.

"We ignore it," I said. "Tumblers have tight schedules. We don't intend to allow our shipment to be delayed."

"You'll take it out? How?"

"Saul, you've seen how large those trains are. Yes?"

"But the navigator. Is he prepared for something like that?"

Vash laughed. "He's trained to deliver on time and not injure Montez property. So, no. He won't like the method we have in mind."

"Huh. Just checking."

Moon continued.

"The Horax will dispatch backup teams in case the blockade fails. They'll assume the tumbler is well defended. They'll come at us from any number of locations in the Brennan Pass."

That's where the business got dicey. Roadway 9 snaked through the Ogala Hills between the largest peaks along the range. Forty-five degree curves were the routine. The train ran at half speed through a ten-kilometer stretch.

"They can choose from hundreds of hiding spots," Vash said. He

107

pointed out some of the most likely. "There aren't many forests in the Ogala range. But this section of old barrontops is a great place to hide rifters, land chasers, and snipers targeting critical systems. It's possible they'll try to hit us with shoulder mounted rockets.

"That's why Ilan's sighter drones will be critical to our success. When we pin down their locations, we shift your locations to different holds to accommodate. We need to hit them with everything we have *before* they rain down on the train. But don't worry. You'll have ample warning. Raul and Ilan will make sure."

He and Moon reviewed our internal communications plan and ran through the scenarios whereby the hatches and sliding doors might be utilized. They devised nine scenarios the Horax might employ to stop the tumbler. They showed our response to each.

Our team lacked the experience to adjust at once to all those possibilities, but success ultimately came down to me and my longtime partner. We were the eyes and ears. Moon positioned himself in the rear cab and Vash in the center.

Ship posed another question.

"Are we guaranteed home-free if we make it through the pass?"

Moon shook his head as Vash responded with a firm "No."

"Whatever forces we escape but don't cripple are bound to follow. How far is an open question. Once we close within twenty kilometers of Machado, the regional traffic probes monitor all transit. Acts of roadway piracy don't happen that close to cities. The response is quick and deadly. And piracy against a Montez train? Soon as those bastards are caught in the crosshairs, they're dead."

"Our goal," I interjected, "will be to eliminate the Horax threat long before we hit the urban zone. We want them to suffer devastating casualties here while losing all their resources along the road. Bodies strewn over seventy kilometers. They expect to send us a message. We will throw it back in their faces and clarify who runs the Naugista Plateau. I don't mean to undercut the amazing work Ilan and Vash have done, but it's important to remember: Though we are acting from a position of defense, we do intend to kill as many of their messengers as we can manage."

"If their blood ain't on the ground," Elian chimed in, "they'll keep coming back until they smash us."

Ship nodded. "Then we got to paint the ground redder than it already is."

Harlan pushed back his chair and grunted.

"Looks to me like a winning plan. Right people stationed at the proper locations. But here's an issue nobody's dared to speak. What if we're wrong about the Horax? What if they don't attack the tumbler or the town? What then?"

Ilan and Vash deferred to me.

"Our source in the Cardinales' organization is highly placed and, if I may say so, impeccable."

Of course, I didn't want to name the Senora. That might provoke too many awkward questions. Lumen, standing behind the bar, steeled her jaws in the obvious hope I'd keep these things vague.

"They intend to hijack our products, kill the leadership of this town, and murder anyone they don't consider of great monetary value. Ilan, Vash, anything you'd like to add?"

The briefing soon ended, and final weapons drills began outside. Our new army didn't stand a chance without the security perimeter Moon and I installed or the protective shell of a Montez road train. But they made me proud given their inexperience.

I promised a thousand-credit bonus to every fighter if we came out of this showdown unscathed. The guarantee wasn't difficult to make given the unlikelihood of such a payout.

Still, I liked our chances. And what a great new page in history.

Desperido, an old frontier town first used as a waystation for early colonists then abandoned for centuries, was about to earn its tiny little dot on the map.

I couldn't wait until the next sunrise. My partner spent the night wired. He savored the massacre that lay ahead. But the icing on the

cake? The third and final front in our war against the Horax?
Moon and I saved that little nugget for ourselves.

13

MANY FOLKS HAVE ACCUSED ME of being insane. On reflection, I can say with great confidence that I only lost my faculties once in two thousand years. On balance, that ain't a bad track record.

I had returned from six years of fighting a hopeless war where I died a few times before regenerating. I was still battling demons from my past, lost a lover, and saw my command stripped away. The new Captain relegated me to a secondary role and gave me the ol' side-eye. Well, I decided to show him what-for.

With a bomb in hand, I threatened to destroy our warship, sending everyone – myself included – straight to hell. Seemed like the best option at the time, which in retrospect confirmed my break from reality.

Turned out to be a strategically wise maneuver. Oh, the new captain took me down with a good swift kick and the warship's crew went on to achieve great fame. Me? I had the surprising good fortune to be sentenced to a "prison pond" on a nasty little moon called Huryo. For several days, I lived naked in a fetid pool of water while being interrogated by a gargantuan gentleman who waddled into place every morning.

He attempted to cleanse my soul by forcing me to confess my

crimes in considerable detail. He achieved the opposite. I left there with an unprecedented clarity about my true nature:

I existed to cause murder and mayhem in pursuit of heroic deeds.

One might call this a contradiction, but I'd disagree. Naturally.

Among my many achievements:

1/ I slaughtered a villainous man and his entire family before he could lead the planet of my childhood down a rabbit hole of madness.

2/ I crossed between universes and killed the Empress of an empire that worshipped a false god and by extension saved young Moon's family from certain extinction.

3/ I trained Moon to become a bloodier killer than I ever was, which paved our eventual rise to godhood.

4/ Moon and I slaughtered the oldest, most advanced species in the universe – thirty million Creators – in order to reset reality to its original, natural state.

Nothing that was about to happen on the Naugista Plateau rose to such grand, intergalactic heights. However, the big three – murder, mayhem, and heroism – dominated the agenda.

Or soon would.

The tumbler arrived on schedule, which meant today's real fun would have to wait until the auditors did their business, and goods were properly exchanged.

Four men in white coveralls, short-bibbed matching hats and dark glasses supervised our shipment. The auditor expressed surprise at the volume, but Lumen (who I allowed to remain as the face of the town) replied that her people had developed a stronger work ethic.

"And a keen nose for profit," the auditor replied. "Your buyers are going to be very pleased."

He handed over the gross revenue projections on the off-book manifest. Lumen showed me the numbers.

One percent above my own estimates. Not bad!

The informal air between the auditor and Lumen made much more sense than the first time I witnessed these transactions. No doubt this man and those who accompanied him from cargo hold three were also Children of Orpheus.

One of them was told what to expect upon arrival — specifically, men and women armed with big guns, unheard of in this dusty little town. Who precisely? Vash wasn't given a name. He and I spoke of our inside contact moments before the tumbler entered town.

"When it's time, he'll facilitate our way onboard," Vash said. "But take care: He's not guild. If the others pick a fight, they won't be inclined to hear him out."

"Will they challenge men with rifles?"

"That boils down to luck of the draw."

I snickered. "Or the dulcet tones of my reassurances. I'd prefer not to use this weapon on anyone *inside* the tumbler."

"That's a good plan, Raul. See you keep to it. Same for Ilan."

As we left the cantina following a final huddle with Ilan and my lieutenants, I pulled Vash aside.

"A question, my friend. How many years have you carried out hits for the Children of Orpheus?"

Naturally, his grimace said I blindsided him.

"What business could that be of yours?"

"Despite our awkward introduction two weeks ago, we *are* men of a similar heritage."

"I doubt it, Raul."

My wagging finger disagreed.

"Our agendas may vary, but we both kill in the name of the greater good. How many years?"

"Ten. And you?"

Now that was a complicated answer. I disregarded the middle nineteen hundred and sixty years.

"Since I was seventeen." His eyes ballooned to some hazy stratosphere between disbelief and newfound respect. "It's opened many doors, though I would only recommend the career choice to a scant few."

"Why are you telling me this, Raul?"

"Because I have an important question."

"Be quick. Tumbler's almost here."

The road train appeared amid the flat red horizon.

"Have you ever regretted killing a man, Vash?"

"If it served our purpose? No. Doesn't mean I don't regret."

He revealed far more than expected. I smiled and slapped him on the shoulder.

"You regret not killing Ilan and me. Yes?"

"Every day, Raul."

He said it with a sly grin.

"I'll make a prediction, Vash."

"What?"

"You and I are going to be lifelong friends."

He walked away, mumbling under his breath.

It was a nice moment. A breakthrough. If he survived today, I planned to follow up. Only a tiny percentage of men engaged in our nefarious business. We saw humanity through a unique prism. Why not share a few war stories?

Later, as the tumbler defense team waited for cargo hold three to be loaded, I studied Ship. The kid seemed a little thin for the rifle he held across his chest, but he watched the proceedings with the earnestness of a young man impatient for battle.

"Any last-minute concerns?" I asked.

"No, boss. I'm good."

"Is your ear bead working?"

He gasped, as if realizing a horrible oversight. Ship tapped his right ear twice.

"I got nothing, boss."

"That," I said with a sardonic twist, "is because we haven't activated them." I rubbed his head for good measure. "Keeping you alert, my friend. We'll go live after we're inside."

I believed in the boy, but we might've given him more than he could chew. Unlike Elian, who already possessed the cold heart I required, Ship was a work in progress. In time, he'd follow Moon's long road and abandon his morals. Unlike Moon, the kid could only die once.

The auditor and Lumen concluded informal banter while the other three loaded several rifters worth of product into the hold. They appeared to receive no help from the guild crewmen.

Interesting.

Was hold three off-limits to the guild? Were they forbidden from assisting with cargo not on the official manifest?

Either way, it slowed departure. The "official resupply" from hold one had yet to begin.

When the rifters emptied, the auditor shook hands with Lumen and turned on his heels military-style. The other three disappeared inside the hold. My team waited for the signal.

The auditor leaped into the open egress, stopped for a beat, and glanced over his shoulder. He lowered his glasses and waved us forward with two fingers.

"Not a surprise," Vash said. "He's our senior man on the inside."

The ten of us hustled thirty meters to the egress.

"Has he told the others?"

"Likely. They didn't flinch when they saw the greeting party."

Moon took lead. I waited until all our people were aboard.

Before jumping up, I offered a sharp salute to Lumen and our spunky militia. Most returned the salute and broke for their stations around town. Lumen and two volunteers to handle the rifters waited like quiet sentinels for the official auditor to open the first hold.

Inside, our auditor pulled a lever at the end of the egress, and the long door slid shut, passing through a series of clamps. When it closed, the clamps locked into place. The seal finalized with a hiss.

The interior impressed me. It had a warehouse feel and was brighter lit than I predicted. The three rows of shelves, storage bins, and cooling units were well organized, with access nodes speckled along the way.

In relation to the navigator's cab, we entered the tumbler's portside, opposite the narrow crew aisle where most of our team would soon be stationed. That's where we'd find access to the maintenance hatches taking us either to the train's underbelly or the roof.

"There's so much," Harlan said. "All this for the night market?"

The auditor removed his glasses. He was a fortysomething with a tiny mustache that appeared drawn above his lip.

"You assumed Desperido was the only town operating off book."

"I did, sir."

Judging from the other nods, these folks apparently thought they had cornered the criminal marketplace.

Nothing like the small-town mindset. Always worth a few giggles.

Vash beamed when he saw the auditor's face.

"Manny Borta? You beautiful malgado! An auditor now?"

They hugged like long-lost brothers.

"A lot has changed in five years, old friend. I wondered what happened to you after the trouble at Ixoca."

"Too long a story." Vash turned to our team. "Manny and I go way back. We're in good hands."

"What about the others?" Moon pointed to the three indies who were storing and registering our products. "Will they keep silent?"

"They will." The auditor waved us forward to a holostation equipped with a pair of tall stools. "I told them everything I knew, which wasn't much. You're here to provide additional security for a route that might prove perilous. I realize you don't have time to go into detail. Once hold one is loaded, this train will pull out. But I need a guarantee that this crew will not be placed in danger."

Vash glanced my way, but I thought it better the auditor hear the truth from a friend.

"We make no guarantees, Manny. But if the crew locks itself in the break rooms, the chance for injury is low. Do you expect trouble from the guild?"

"Hard to say. They follow the Nav's orders."

"Then," I interjected, "there will be no trouble." I reached out my hand. "Raul Torreta. I'll be in consultation with the Nav."

"Good luck. She's a difficult coit."

I allowed my rifle to linger at my side. No need for threats.

Yet.

"Fortunately, I've dealt with many women of power, my friend. They've all fallen for my considerable charm."

The auditor raised his brow in an are-you-for-real? twist. Either he considered me delusional or thought I was an arrogant asshole. I supposed both could be true at once.

"Piece of advice, Raul. Her name is MaryBeth, but she prefers Bett, and a man with a Mark 11 blast rifle is not going to charm her, no matter your tactics. Be quick and to the point."

"Advice heard. Thank you."

"I have work to finish," Manny told our team. "We'll leave soon."

Moon stepped forward.

"After we begin moving, how long before they clear the aisle?"

"Desperido's an easy delivery. Wait two minutes then make your moves. Best chance to avoid resistance."

The auditor went about his business while our team gathered into a circle to run over last-minute details.

Moon activated our ear beads, which we tested. Ship glanced at me sheepishly when he realized it now worked.

"Headsets," Moon said.

We slipped on wide, single-frame glasses, which attached nicely over one ear. I created them by extracting small grams of my syneth, which used a design template from my time fighting that hopeless war in another universe. I used Bart's autocomm system to build in trackers similar to what my sedan utilized while jaunting across the galaxy.

I opened my pom and tossed out our critical holos, which included the train's schematics and the regional topography. I tapped the headset, which allowed the holos to spread across our little network.

"Everyone see clearly?" I asked.

Nods all around. Perfect.

I asked everyone to focus on the train. Our firepower was to be concentrated close to the accordion-like bridges that connected the holds. Smart attackers had to know those areas were the most vulnerable. The maintenance hatches ran adjacent.

"As soon as we enter the base of the hills, I'll contact everyone from Nav. After we pass through the first obstacle, you'll climb to the upper hatch. We must target the enemy with precision before they have a chance to inflict a crippling blow to this train. Questions?"

Moon quickly hit key principles but avoided details. It was too late for anyone to back out or engage in a dress rehearsal. They knew their shit or they didn't.

"And please, remember who we're fighting," Vash said. "The train's crew is here to do a job. They're not the enemy. They have families."

"If any of them do decide to play Fast-Gun Jose," I added, "force them back into their break room."

Vash nodded. "The shipping guild is powerful. If they lose people in a bloodbath, they'll stop working this route. Good luck sending your products to the global night market. And offworld? Forget it."

The long-range data from our sighter drones confirmed what we would have to face.

"As expected, they're moving their pieces into position," I said. "They're playing a predictable game. We are not, my friends. That gives us the advantage, though it does not guarantee victory. Everyone must do your job. No gaps."

"Yes, boss," said Ship, louder than the rest. "We got this."

I so liked the kid. All that potential bottled up in an untested bundle of well-meaning ambition. I so hoped he didn't get himself killed.

Right after Ship spoke, the road train lurched northward.

14

TWO MINUTES LATER, WE MOVED OUT. The starboard aisles were a meter wide and sparsely lit. We heard the rumble of those mammoth wheels directly beneath us. My team spread in opposite directions. Moon lead most south toward the end of hold three and onward to the first two holds and the now-rear navigation cab. The transition hub to the bridge glowed around its seal as they passed through. Only Vash remained, taking his station there.

Time to set the table.

I led Harlan, Saul, and Genoa (a soft-spoken woman with a crewcut and the steadiest trigger finger in the militia) toward hold four, the last stop before the current Nav cab.

"Saul, take position," I said.

He quickly studied the maintenance hatch next to the bridge. The rest of us passed through, a brief but unsettling experience. In its typical transit state, the bridge maintained a tight link, only a meter between holds. However, it flexed as the various laws of physics demanded. It could stretch up to five meters. Thus, the floor did not feel stable.

Our mission threatened to derail the instant we entered hold one.

Two crewmen — I assumed guild — advanced toward us. They

froze upon seeing our weapons. Why weren't they in the break room?

Neither wore glasses or caps.

"Good day," I said, hoping the man in front wasn't reaching for a weapon. "If you would, please retreat to a safe location. We're not here to harm anyone."

The woman behind mumbled, but I heard: "Pirates."

"We're additional security, paid by Montez to assure your cargo speeds safely through a precarious route. Now, please retreat. There will be no violence if you cooperate."

"Liar. Ja, he's a ..."

I didn't aim my weapon, but I did adjust it against my chest. It seemed poised for action. The man in front swung about and whispered to our accuser.

He effectively pushed her toward the break room.

Genoa took her position at the first hatch. I led Harlan forward, five meters behind our concerned passengers.

They disappeared into the break room but not without glancing back, their terror as evident as their rage. The door had not yet slid shut when I passed. A quick study found six humans inside, one of whom was the auditor, Manny Borta. He glared at me with a perplexed grimace, as if he knew more than he could say. Half the crew – some guild – were gathered here within fifteen feet of the cab.

I saw a potential for trouble, so I stepped into the threshold.

"I'll keep it simple. Remain where you are, and we'll soon be gone. Leave this room before your Nav delivers an all-clear, and I can't guarantee you'll see the end of your three-day shift."

Eyes narrowed to slits, jaws hung loose, and much to my pleasant surprise, no one asked a stupid question. As we pushed forward, Harlan said:

"Are you sure about them, Raul?"

The break room door slid shut.

"No, Harlan. You and Genoa should keep a close eye.

Understood?"

"On it, boss."

He stationed himself at the final maintenance hatch.

"Oh, and Harlan. Just a thought. You'll take twenty years off if you shave that beard."

He chuckled. I was not the first to mock his beard.

I proceeded through the forward bridge into the navigator's cab. The woman piloting this train sat in a shallow well surrounded by tempered glass screens of diagnostics and maps. Jaunty music filled the cab from side speakers. The Nav, whose black hair was pressed into a tight bun, ate an apple while she reviewed the data.

Bett, as the crew called her, did not see me enter from her blind spot. I took the occasion to size up my options. The primary Nav controls jutted forward between the monitors. Bett needed only to lean in a few inches to grab the arms and alter the train's speed or heading. The cab wasn't designed for a co-navigator. If I wanted to make drastic adjustments to our course, Bett would have to follow instructions, or I'd have to kill her.

I preferred to avoid the latter option. I'd lose all mobility if I had to take over Nav.

"Good morning," I greeted Bett. She swiveled about in quite a fright (perfectly understandable) but lost her apple.

Odd. Did no one ever surprise her with a visit up here?

"Who in the ten hells are you?"

"Settle, my friend. Allow your hands to remain where I can see them. I'm not interested in hurting you or any of your crew."

"How did you get onboard my ...?"

She seethed. Was it my sudden appearance or the lack of a warning from her crew? Hmm. I might've expected one of those fools in the break room to think faster.

"Hold three. *Borta*. That fucking malg ..."

"Please. Be at peace. Now, I'm sure you have a weapon stowed within reach. A Stahl Mark 9. Or something more interesting. Yes? I assure you my reflexes are nonpareil. Do not test them. For the sake of a pleasant engagement, I'd like you to face forward and follow my instructions."

Violence wasn't new to this woman. A scar snaked across her left forehead, and her nearest eye wasn't the original.

"I knew Borta couldn't be trusted. I warned the company about him. In league with pirates. Motherfuc ..."

"Pirates? Oh, Bett. Not at all. Senor Borta did facilitate my team's entry, but we're not here to steal from you. On the contrary, we intend to keep you alive and this train on course without delay."

She laughed with no hint of irony.

"Do not take me for the town idiot."

"Of course not. But in the spirit of accommodation, please follow my first instruction. Face forward."

I took position behind her. Did she expect me to shoot her in the back? Reckoned I might if I were a pirate.

No, I preferred to see my victim's eyes before the kill shot.

When she complied, I took a few seconds to study the road ahead. The Ogala Hills filled the massive windshield. We'd reach the critical choke point within ten minutes at current speed.

"Tell me what you want," she said.

"Trust. I realize that's a difficult ask given the circumstances but essential to saving your crew and this train. We boarded to protect you from an imminent attack. Without our assistance, this train will be wrecked, its cargo stolen – especially the profitable items in hold three – and the crew terminated."

I wasn't sure about the last bit, but upon further consideration, it made sense. A full-on slaughter would force the Montez group to shut down this route until the government authorized security forces. That would draw a spotlight on Desperido and crush the town's economy.

"You've lost your mind. Nobody would be insane enough to take out a Montez train."

"Not insane. Annoyed. You're familiar with the Horax?"

Bett started to swivel around, but I aimed my rifle.

"They wouldn't dare."

"Look ahead, Bett. What do you see?" When she hesitated for a beat, I added: "It's not a trick question."

"I see the fucking road."

"And beyond it?"

"Ogala Hills."

"Which would be an outstanding location for an ambush."

Bett crimped her fists into fighting mode. Oh, she so wanted to reach for her hidden weapon.

"That's where *your* people are waiting."

"Not mine."

I flipped open my pom and tore off the topographical holo.

"Here's a gift." She grabbed the drifting holo. "Go ahead. Select the nearest marker. You'll see live images from a sighter drone."

She tapped the marker half a kilometer into the southern edge of the Ogala range, where Roadway 9 curved forty degrees and left little room to maneuver.

"Fuck me."

Indeed. Three vehicles blockaded the road. Men with rifles and a shoulder-supported missile launcher waited.

"Please don't overreact, Bett. Your first inclination will be ..."

She didn't hesitate to tap the glass monitor to her left. It tracked the train's course. She slid her fingers toward the open desert.

"I think not." Bett stiffened when I shoved the rifle into the back of her neck. "Remain on course."

"I knew it. They're *your* people."

"No, but going overland will require a significant detour, costing you precious time. Plus, if you deviate, the Horax will detect your course change. They'll follow, and they will be relentless."

"Wha ...? Y-you expect to me to ..."

"Run the blockade. Yes."

124

Bett retracted her hand before initiating the course change.

"Not a chance."

"You have a snow smasher for northern winter routes. Deploy it."

"The snow ...?"

"Now, please."

"You won't leave my train alive. Hear me?"

"The name is Raul. I enjoy whiskey, and I'd love to share a glass with you when our adventure concludes. Death would render that celebration moot. Deploy the snow smasher."

We'd begin a slight ascent into the hills any moment now.

Bett chose wisely. She tapped the control monitor to her right. A wide blade emerged from beneath the cab, stretching forth on a pair of arms.

"Beautiful. Now, open a channel to your crew and prepare them for a turbulent ride. Assure them there is no danger and to remain in their quarters until you signal the all-clear."

She disobeyed my first order and glared over her shoulder.

"Time is short," I said. "They need to hear from their Nav."

"Do they? How many did you bring onto my train?"

"Ah. You think they should fight. Perhaps you'll order them to."

Bett said nothing, but her good eye suggested that the idea crossed her mind.

"Your injuries," I said. "Did you acquire them in service for Montez, or elsewhere?"

"This is wrong. I won't do it."

"Now you're engaging in bravado for the sheer sake of it. How stupid. The Swarm war. Yes. That's where you lost your eye."

Why didn't I see it in the beginning? She carried herself with the demeanor of a former soldier.

"UNF?" I asked.

"I flew Hornets. I killed dozens of those malgados. You don't frighten me, Raul."

I could've told her my partner and I saved the Collectorate from

125

those nasty invaders in our final act as true gods. That we were heroes the public never knew about.

No. Too long a conversation.

"You're not at war, Bett. Make the smart choice. Now."

She plotted the odds. Might she grab that pistol fast enough to end this madness before it began?

And then she surrendered. More or less. If nothing else, she was a practical woman. I liked practical in my humans.

Bett tapped the train-wide comm.

"Crew, this is Nav. We have some rough weather up ahead. Hang where you are until I say otherwise, and no one gets hurt. Nav out."

"Well done, Bett. Now, eyes on the road."

I tapped my ear bead.

"Attention, team. Our pilot has proven quite courteous. We're less than two minutes from the blockade. When you feel the inevitable jolt, proceed to the next phase. Raul out."

"Next phase? What are you people planning?"

"Like I told you before, the defense of this train and its cargo. We're fighting our own little war of sorts. You just happen to be an involuntary observer."

Her shoulders remained stiff as dried mortar, yet I sensed a resignation that she'd have to see this through. Still ...

"You'll never escape justice, Raul. If that's your name."

"Bett, I too fought Swarm. I wasn't UNF. Worked for a different outfit. Ground ops."

"Empathy? *Really?* That's your play?"

"Not at all. I was going to make a simple observation. I despised the Swarm more than anyone in this universe. They were the existential enemy. In the end, we won. But war never truly ends. It never leaves your blood. Peace is a manifestation of false hope. We see enemies everywhere. You believe I'm the enemy because this rifle is inches from the back of your head. But in truth, your foe lies around the next curve. Accept that reality, and you will live. What else matters?"

I didn't anticipate spewing that little nugget of philosophy at such a critical moment, yet it felt well-timed.

"A *simple* observation?" She said.

"Manage your train, Bett. Make good choices."

As we approached the curve, Bett lessened the train's velocity but not below the projected speed through this segment of the route.

The train rounded its way into the base of the hills.

There they were.

Revenge of the Horax.

"Do not slow down, Bett."

"They're armed. If they start firing ..."

"The glass is six inches thick and reinforced. Yes?"

"I'm more worried about keeping her stable on impact."

Hills sloped sharply up either side of Roadway 9, a perfect location for mayhem. The train could not barrel around the blockade, nor did our Horax friends leave themselves an easy escape route.

"If you flew Hornets, you must have attacked Swarm war cruisers. How life-threatening are these morons by comparison?"

"This is no UNF fighter. I can't change course in here."

"Point taken."

At current speed, we'd ram them in fifteen seconds. These assholes weren't moving. Did they think a fifty-meter road train stopped on a dime? Had they reached the stage of mumbled curses? Wondering who'd give the order to run like hell?

"Steady on, Bett. Welcome to our war."

Nine seconds. Eight. Seven.

Move, morons.

One idiot fired a rifle. A few laser blasts impacted the glass and bounced off.

Cardinale's people jumped.

In all my adventures, I had never run a blockade. I intended to enjoy this one.

15

NICE. AN OFF-ROAD RACER FLIPPED, two sedans designed for genteel city driving lost their front ends, and three humans too stupid for words launched skyward. One smashed into the cab's windshield then slid away like a mindless insect, leaving a thin trail of blood.

The tumbler shuddered as Bett maintained firm control of the Nav arms. I watched the chaotic scene unfold from our sighter drone. The Horax thugs who escaped a quick death recouped well enough to lay down fire on the final two cargo holds before the tail passed through their foolhardy blockade.

After the fifty-meter train cleared the site, survivors hopped on rifters and pursued. We expected as much. Moon would handle those animals from a perch above the rear cab.

"Tell me that's the end of it," Bett said.

"New challenges lie ahead, I fear. No worries, my friend. We have them covered."

I tapped my ear bead and spoke to the team.

"That wonderful vibration you experienced was the sound of assholes playing in the road. Ascend to the roof. Monitor your headset for snipers. Hit them first. Raul out."

Bett shifted her gaze between the system diagnostics and the topographical holo, which pinpointed multiple red markers over the next forty kilometers.

"All for this train?"

"Have you ever dealt with the Horax before?"

"I don't associate with criminals."

"I do. Often. Usually, with somewhat deleterious consequences. What we have today is a family-run business seeking retribution for the loss of family members. Not blood relatives, mind you. Not most, anyway. We didn't actually test their gene stamps."

Perhaps I said too much. A habit of mine.

Bett stared at me like I was a Swarm soldier in need of a good, swift flash peg to the head.

"You brought my crew into the middle of that?"

"Yes. My partner and I. At any rate, we have a few moments until the next round of fun. Did the tumbler sustain damage?"

"Scratches and burn marks."

"Superficial. Good. I trust Montez won't dock your credits?"

She cursed roundly under her breath; some words I'd never heard before. Perhaps jargon she picked up during her UNF service.

"If they do, I'll send you a bill."

"Might be difficult, Bett. I tend to move around."

The good lady snarled at me.

"I've traveled every kilometer of this rock. I'll find you."

I saw it in those deep brown eyes (albeit one slightly larger than the other): This woman was goal-oriented. Stand in her way at your peril.

"I don't doubt it."

She immersed herself in the data for a few quiet seconds then said barely loud enough for me to hear:

"For argument's sake, what will we face at those next markers?"

"Expect variety. Since they know we're onto them, they'll show no mercy. The blockade was a gentleman's way to pillage. That's why it failed. They thought it might, hence the many backup plans."

I admired humans who didn't set their fate to a single option.

"One well-targeted missile could rip us apart, Raul, and they have the high ground."

"Correct on both counts." I pointed to the twenty small green blips spaced throughout the Ogala Hills. "Our sighter drones will reveal themselves when the train moves within range of enemy weapons. Each drone will emit a repetitive, high-pitched shrill as it closes in on the target."

"A distraction?"

"Indeed. At the same instant, my team will use the drone's data to target the enemy and lay down heavy covering fire. This combination will greatly reduce their strategic advantage."

Bett dropped her dismissive side-eye. I saw her military mindset working overtime.

"There's merit, but your people must be precise."

"Our goal is to destroy the enemy, but some will dodge our fire. Even now, remnants from the blockade are pursuing us. My partner has engaged them. Stubborn assholes."

She ran her finger through the holo, tapping on a specific cluster of red markers.

"Most are situated in the Branner Pass. These positions ... they're too protected. Blast rifles won't cause them a bother."

"We have many toys."

Bett flicked me a skeptical glance. She was likely as impressed as she was disgusted. No doubt, she'd demand Montez review its security procedures going forward. How easily we had slipped onto her train!

"Your toys will be put to the test in about eight minutes."

"Steady on, Bett. When it's over, you'll have a story to tell your children someday. Not as thrilling as attacking a Swarm war cruiser, but a close second. Yes?"

She didn't seem amused. Can't please everyone.

I opened my bead to the team.

"We're less than eight minutes from full exposure, my friends. Continue monitoring the way ahead. Strike before they do." I double-tapped the bead to focus on my partner. "How goes it back there?"

"You were right. This is fun. Just took out a rifter."

Moon's spirited voice intermingled with the backdrop of weapons fire from his post atop the rear cabin.

"You always enjoyed target practice in the old days."

"I'll give them credit. They don't back down."

"The worst humans never do. Polish them off before we hit the gauntlet. It's coming up fast, my friend."

I switched back to the broad channel just in time to hear:

"... it's not right .. Raul ... wa ..."

That was Harlan. In distress.

I thought.

Thought.

Too much damn thinking. Assuming.

I was blind.

A bolt of hot gas cut through my side like a blade held over the fire. I lost my footing and fell back against the portside bulwark.

A second bolt caught me south of my syneth ribs.

How?

How did I miss it?

My assassin had slipped into the cab on the quiet feet of a true professional. He was decked in white coveralls, his features disguised beneath a short-bib hat and dark glasses of a Montez shipping agent.

"Raul!" He shouted, firing again.

One. Two. Three blasts.

I pulled myself together and leapt ahead on the last drops of adrenaline my syneth core could provide. One shot hit me in a lung, but I avoided the others.

On a good day, I ran fifty times faster than the average human. In this instant, my collapsing body was lucky to push a third that speed.

Instinct raised my weapon and lifetimes of experience fired it.

My aim was true. I shredded my assassin with a barrage of flash pegs. He danced a fatal jig, his rifle firing in every direction. Its laser bolts ricocheted off the cab walls.

Then he fell in a heap.

How did I not see this coming?

I dropped to my knees.

"Theo. This ... this ain't good. Pull the reserves from my syneth core. Hurry."

My *D'ru-shaya* gasped like a man in desperate need of oxygen.

"I'm ... trying. You ... you're all torn up ... dumbass."

I removed my free hand from the chest wound. My fingers were doused in red blood. OK. A good sign, actually.

If only ...

Shit.

The red synthetic liquid thinned. It transformed into a wet, runny silver syneth. It did not coagulate with true syneth properties, the kind that allowed me to create new objects, shapeshift, or regenerate body parts. Worse: I hurt all over.

"C'mon, Theo. Please, my friend. I need you. We're dying."

He didn't respond. Had the trauma already taken him? If so, I'd dissolve within minutes.

Two thousand years of incredible lives reduced to a silver slime.

No. Not yet. Not this way.

My arm felt like it was broken, but I raised it against my ear and tapped the bead twice.

"I've been shot. I'm fucked up, partner. I need you."

He didn't respond either.

I heard a moan in the navigation well but lacked the energy to stand. On top of everything else ...

"Bett?"

Goddamn. Must've been a ricochet.

The train. All it had to do was miss one of the many upcoming curves and we'd lose on every count.

133

"Theo? Talk to me, buddy. What's happening in there? What do you see? What do ...?"

His wheezing echoed through my brain.

"I found the reserves. They're ... a-almost gone."

"Start with the lung. That one will kill me the fastest. Try to ..."

Moon raced into the cab, a burn mark under his left shoulder, rifle aimed. He bent down beside me.

"I'm sorry, my friend. I didn't see it coming."

I'd always been good at reading Moon, who usually wavered somewhere between rage and simmering rage. But his eyes squinted when he saw my wounds. My face shifted beneath my skin, struggling to hold the form of Raul Torreta.

Was that fear I saw? For the first time since we became gods, my onetime protégé was afraid.

He set down his rifle.

"It was a trap," he said, glancing at the dead assassin. "One came after me, too. Harlan's dead."

Harlan? So much for shaving that damn beard.

My words fell with long spaces in between.

"Horax ... planted ... onboard. I never ... saw it. Why?"

"What am I supposed to do, Royal?"

The great serpent god sounded like a lost boy. I experienced a fleeting image of Moon unchained, wreaking havoc on the universe without me to keep him in check.

He'd kill everyone onboard for starters.

"Theo's ... trying to ... Moon ... check on ... Nav. The train is ..."

He nodded and glanced into the well.

"She was hit but she's alive. Hands on the controls."

OK. One positive. But how bad was she hurt? If she lost consciousness and the train's AI didn't compensate ...

"Other ... Nav. Bring ... forward."

Assuming the navigator who piloted the tumbler into Desperido wasn't one of the assassins, we had little choice. Moon didn't agree.

"You first, Royal. How do I save you?"

We never talked in specifics about field triage in the unlikely event one of us took a mortal wound. That job fell to our *D'ru-shayas*. They'd handle anything shy of annihilation.

"Progress, Theo?"

"I can siphon enough reserves to rebuild respiration, old man. There ain't enough for the rest. It has to come from Moon."

"I knew you'd say that. Asshole."

"If you don't do it, Royal, I'll scream us to our death, you worthless piece of shit."

What choice did I have?

When I was a biological immortal, I took many kill shots, usually comforted in the knowledge I'd regenerate within ten to twelve minutes. My creators designed me that way. After every death, I sank into a place that felt like a dark hole of no return, where the worst memories became an eternal reality. Unlike mortals, my visits were short. Life reached down and rescued me.

I doubted there was any reality waiting after the last of my syneth dissolved. Would my consciousness flitter off into the vast universe? Or would I see a blackout curtain fall over all my grand adventures?

"Need ... yours ..."

The words were harder to articulate. *Words*. Beautiful, twisting, poetic, elegant, gorgeous words. My stock in trade.

Dying. I bolloxed everything.

"You need my syneth?" Moon asked. "How much?"

I asked Theo the same question.

"Ninety percent of his reserves, Royal."

"No. I already took his humanity. I won't ..."

"Shut up, old man. This ain't the time to moralize. We are about to disappear into the goddamn ether. You listening?"

"How long will it take for him to rebuild his reserves?"

"That's a question for Addis, and I don't have the strength to talk to her. Years, at the least. Do it, Royal. Take his reserves."

135

"He'll be as vulnerable as a human."

Theo laughed at the absurd irony. I didn't blame him.

"He already was. Same as you, Royal. You're living like them now. Get used to it, dumbass."

Who was I kidding? I had always put myself before anyone else. That's how survivors played the great game. What chance would I see the error of my ways in the face of my final death?

Yeah, no.

"Your ... reserves," I told Moon. "Need ... reserves."

"Anything, partner. How much?"

He'd be fine. Moon could destroy an army on his own.

"All," I told him. "All ... reserves."

I don't know whether he understood the implication or even cared. What followed proved his undying love, which I always knew he hid in those little backrooms of his human consciousness.

His hands morphed into pure syneth.

"Tell him to apply directly to your wounds," Theo said.

I pointed rather than spoke.

The silver skin, made up of the most astonishing organic compounds ever devised, seeped into my body as if reaching for a new home. We were the last two sources of pure syneth in all Creation. We were built on a formula so valuable we made sure the human race never acquired its secrets. Any species to do so might rise to godhood; why we would share that space in the mythology of future generations?

The effects weren't instantaneous. I still felt broken all over. Every synthetic muscle and bone agonized. Theo had to direct the syneth into my core and reallocate it to restore all my functions.

When Moon's hands reconstituted, he grabbed his rifle.

"Will it work? Do you need more, partner?"

"No. Give ... time."

His frightened tone returned to the more traditional rage.

"I'll kill them all, Royal."

"No." I grabbed him with what felt like a shattered arm. "Need other Nav. Still ... have ... to fight Horax."

He pointed to the dead man.

"You know what this means, right?"

I nodded. "Yeah. But ... not ... not yet, Moon. Deal with them ... later. Get other Nav."

How much time had passed? No doubt it was less than I imagined, but precariously close to disaster.

"Go," I spat my words. "Other Nav. Hurry."

He raced from the cab in a blur.

I felt enough strength to clamber to my knees and stumbled over to the assassin. I removed his glasses. We met him in the aisle of hold four. A woman behind him called us pirates.

The identity wasn't important. I'd deal with that crap later.

Now felt like the time for a pity party.

Not only had certain victory been reduced to grave uncertainty, but I opened the door to this disaster.

I didn't see it coming.

How in the name of the nine universes did I overlook this one?

16

IN THE FINAL CENTURY BEFORE we ascended, Moon and I learned the language of the gods. *Quesh-n'o.* Without it, we never would've made sense of the chemical properties that formed syneth. We spoke in musical tones and clicks. All the while, we lived inside an enclosed world called the Origin. Five light-years long, free from time itself. We defied every damn law of physics.

All those centuries. All that fun.

Then we gave up our human bodies. Syneth replicated them and assimilated our consciousness. Syneth architecture and fluent *Quesh-n'o* allowed us to conquer time itself, to change our form, and jump across the continuum to wherever we pleased.

The headiest of days. We controlled everydamnthing.

Humans lived at our discretion. Planets revolved around stars if we left them alone.

We learned every spoken language in nine universes.

The name on our storefront would've been Omnipotent Central.

Syneth was exactly what our mentors billed: Beautiful and horrifying in equal doses. We tapped into both.

It seemed like the gift we'd never part with. But we made an unshakeable deal: Reset reality, allow humans to see life as it was always meant to be, long before the Creators built their own. That was one hell of a deal.

Cost us nearabout everything.

Now, the syneth was all that sustained us. *Quesh-n'o* faded from memory when we landed on Azteca. The recipe to defy time went with it. We weren't human for damn sure, but I reckoned we weren't quite as superior as our egos claimed.

I rose to my feet in the navigator's cab and checked on Bett. A river of drool dribbled from the corner of her mouth. Her eyes fluttered, but she wasn't unconscious. Her hands gripped the control arms. The train swerved across the lanes.

Fortunately, she had Roadway 9 to herself at the moment.

"Bett, you there? You with me?"

My so-called body still felt like leftovers, but the words crossed my lips with less space between them. Not so for the Nav.

"Can't ... hold. Help."

I gripped the railing behind the well, uncertain how far I could walk on my own. The new syneth coursed through my replicated organs and bloodstream, but my innards took one gut punch after another.

"Move it!"

I heard Moon a second before he pushed a man into the cab.

"Take the controls," he insisted.

This fella was younger and svelte. He seemed better suited as a streaming model than a long-haul shipping navigator. He turned pale when he saw Bett's state and rushed into the well.

"Bett. Bett, what did they do to you?"

"Nothing," I growled. "Blame your dead friend. Take the controls. We're coming up on a nasty curve."

The Nav quickly assessed the monitors.

"Cudfrucker."

"Take the control arms. Now. Moon, grab her."

"No," the Nav said. "She's hurt bad. She was hit near the heart."

Fair point. But what could we do? This train was about to reach the end of the line.

"Do you have a phasic trauma pod onboard?"

This Nav was a baby compared to Bett.

"Y-yeah. Yes. Forward break room."

Moon knew my orders before I gave them. He swooped in, pushed past the new Nav, and grabbed Bett.

"There. Now. Keep us on course. Do not slow down the train. Hear me, kid?"

"Y-yes, sir. I ... I ..."

"Sit and do your damn job."

Had I screwed the pooch one last time? Maybe Bett could've handled the curve in her diminished state. She was a tough coit, for sure. This mess did not fall on her shoulders.

"Oh .... oh ...."

The new Nav led us into the curve ...

And up the slope.

"Oh ... Mother, I'm sorry. I'm so sorry."

Shit. The little asshole was preparing to die.

"Correct course. Do it!"

I held the rail, while Moon stumbled toward me, Bett dangling inside his arms.

The cab tilted to port at twenty degrees. Thirty. Forty.

Don't you dare. Not after everything. Not now.

This time, the laws of physics were not on our side. And us without the magic to defy them.

I rarely saw land from this cockeyed angle.

The Nav was shaken to the core (perfectly understandable), but he knew his job well. He worked with the train's AI to steady itself across the rough terrain. The cab bounced and shook as we reached fifty degrees and then, because the timeline never said we'd die today, the train reestablished contact with the roadway.

The Nav whooped.

"Oh ... oh, sweet heavens! We're good. She's steady."

And under fire. We had entered the Branner Pass. Gentle slopes quickly morphed into steep hillsides, with a blend of rocky terrain and scrub brush.

"Moon, get her to the trauma pod. We have to check on our people and preempt these targets." I focused on Bett. Her eyes were open, although I wasn't sure she was still truly with me.

"Keep it together, Bett. You survived Swarm cruisers. You'll come out the other side."

She didn't respond as Moon carried her away.

"Nav, what's your name?"

"N-Nestor, sir."

"Open a channel, Nestor. Tell your crew: Next one who raises a weapon against us will die a horrible death."

"What? You want me to say what?"

"Repeat my words. Now."

"Yes, sir."

He opened the internal comm and delivered the message, more or less according to instruction.

I needed to check in with my people. Were they still alive? Had they held to their stations? Were they taking fire?

My hands were empty.

The pom. Where's my pom?

No luck searching my pockets. For a second, I had a terrible feeling it had been struck by a laser bolt. Closed, it might have survived the impact. But it was in my hands, flipped open and projecting a holo when ...

I searched portside first. It would've rolled that way at the curve.

Only my rifle laid against the bulwark. My legs carried me to it, but each step felt like a slog in knee-high mud.

"Theo, update. How much longer before I'm fully restored?"

"Fully, old man? Forget it. We're lucky to be alive, no thanks to your incompetence."

"You don't need to remind me, but I'm sure you will to the end of our days."

Theo chuckled with relish. The bastard lost none of his qualities.

"Your organ repair is almost complete. The core pulled from your ambulatory regulators to keep you functioning until it took on Moon's reserves. The new syneth ain't a straight-up swap. It was designed for Moon. Now it has to reconfigure. Patience, dumbass."

"Simple question, Theo. How long?"

"Out of my control."

That didn't sound right. *D'ru-shayas* were AIs built to act as syneth managers inside physical bodies. Theo was a pain in the ass since he gained a personality, but he took care to advise me how much syneth I'd dispense to create objects whole-cloth. He'd redistribute syneth to keep levels steady and sustainable no matter the stress I placed on my system. He did most of that work in the background, free of complaint. Now I wondered: Had this bastard deceived me?

I saved that discussion for another time and tapped my ear bead.

"Talk to me, team. Are we taking fire?"

It was a stupid question, something unfamiliar to me. Of course we were taking fire, as the exterior explosions and laser blasts confirmed.

"We're knocking out their positions before they shoot," Vash said. "Most of the trouble is coming from behind. They're regrouping and striking from the rear."

"No worries, boss," Ship said. "They ain't made a solid strike yet. I had my first hit, boss."

"Great, kid. Keep your focus. We'll toast your kills later. Genoa, Saul, report."

"Vash is right," Saul said. "The drones are doing their thing. We're hitting them hard soon as they're in range, but the ones we miss are coming around for a late pass. We need to reinforce the tail."

"Agree," Genoa said.

"Moon, what's your status?"

142

He breathed like a man gasping for air.

"On my way. Loaded the Nav into the trauma pod." He paused for a beat. "I'll shore up the tail."

"Steady on, my friends. We've got a ways to go yet."

I tapped off the bead.

"Theo, you heard Moon. What the hell's wrong with him?"

"You emptied his reserves while his core was replenishing his wound."

"You told me to."

"I said ninety percent, Royal. You cleaned him out."

Nothing I could say to that.

"Is he in danger?"

"Only if he gets shot up like you. Then he's history. Happy, you selfish ass?"

I tuned out Theo and focused on the road ahead.

"Nav."

"Y-yes, sir?"

"You said your name's Nestor?"

"Nestor Maquilas, sir."

"Listen to me. If I'm reading your map correctly, we got about three kilometers until the next sharp bend. Lock the controls to maintain course straight down the center of Roadway 9. Then look around the well for a golden pom."

"A pom, sir?"

I aimed my rifle. "Follow orders. Don't waste time."

He nodded like a kid scared shitless, which I considered a bonus. Unlike Bett, this Nav lacked a defiant streak.

Nestor scored fast brownie points. He held up my pom not five seconds after his search began.

I lowered my rifle and flipped open the pom, hoping it hadn't been damaged. The critical holos returned.

A quick study of the upcoming roadway demonstrated trouble.

The Horax had repositioned themselves: Three sniper nests were

143

waiting at the next bend. I tapped into the sighter drones and took stock of their weaponry then tapped my ear bead.

"Team: Focus everything you've got on the upcoming nests. Ilan, you'll have to handle the rear attacks yourself. Are you good?"

"Yes, Raul. I'll finish them."

Moon sounded less exhausted.

"Team: I count six shoulder-mounted Ramshorn missile launchers. If one gets through, it will decimate the forward cab."

Nestor jumped.

"Missiles? Wait! What's happening?"

"The Swarm would've killed you in the first seconds. Nestor, purse your lips and do your job. Team, shift your firing mode, acquire targets, and hit them hard with your SE darts."

We didn't carry mere rifles. Moon and I modified them to launch Scorch Eaters. Those nasty little buggers turned brutal ground combat into an over-the-top slaughterfest. Unlike bullets, laser bolts, or flash pegs, Scorch Eaters were hunter-seekers. They targeted coordinates fed into a micro-guidance nodule. Every thumb-sized projectile had a range of three kilometers and the ability to circumvent obstacles.

At impact, an Eater released an accelerant that burned everything inside a ten-meter radius. They were great for stationary targets but worked best fired from cannons. Our proposition – shaky rifles handled by a mobile militia in its first-ever combat – was a bit dicey. My people had to achieve coordinate lock on their headset and pair it with the guidance feature Moon and I added to the rifles. They had trained on the technique for a few days with middling results.

The add-on magazine allowed ten darts per rifle, so we had to be selective. Ordering a barrage on these next targets might expend too much of our firepower before we reached the later choke points. The risk felt necessary.

"Heads up, Nestor."

"Yes, sir?"

"There's a thirty percent chance you'll die in the next minute. Don't panic. Seven in ten chance your beautiful face will remain intact."

There he went with the rapid breathing again. I tore off the holo and expanded the approaching bend for Nestor.

"If you see an inbound missile, take evasive action. Veer the cab sharply left as fast as you can without risking a jackknife. I can't guarantee we'll skirt impact, but it will improve the odds. Eighty-twenty sounds better. Yes?"

His eyes darted between me, the holo, and his controls on tempered glass. Already, he wiped sweat from his brow. Shit.

"Settle, my friend. You're licensed to operate a Montez road train, correct?"

"Yes, sir."

"Time to behave like a professional. Put your hazard training to good use."

"I'll ... uh ... I'll try."

"You'll do better than that."

Bett would've handled this moment with a steel spine and a few choice words for me. I enjoyed making her acquaintance, even if it was fleeting.

I tracked more than a dozen Scorch Eaters launched from our positions along the train. At first, they appeared headed toward collision with the steep, rocky hills due ahead. Then they switched altitude like a graceful symphony rising toward a crescendo.

They had the right idea, clearly headed in the proper direction. But would they consume the targets before these Horax bastards fired? With luck, those snipers atop the Pass were also new to this combat deal.

But I knew better than to count on luck.

This time, I considered every possible outcome.

Lesson learned.

17

THE HILLSIDE ERUPTED with yellow blossoms. Two enemy nests were incinerated before they realized we had a fix on them. Yeah, these guys weren't combat veterans. But I'd bet Desperido that these dearly departed were cocky assholes. And why not? Positioned fifty meters above the road, no idea what was headed their way.

I couldn't say the same for the third nest, which fired a hefty barrage as we rounded the bend.

Three missiles. Five seconds to react.

Nestor tapped the left-side monitor and jerked the control arms. I held tight to the rail and took offense at the possibility of sustaining mortal wounds again so soon. I put my faith in the skills of a twentysomething pretty-boy.

The first missile screamed past in a narrow miss. Meantime, Nestor struggled to stabilize the route, sending the portside off the edge of the roadway, scraping against the ledge.

"Oh ... oh ... Mother."

Not that again.

The second missile impacted in the road's center, where we would have been otherwise. I dared to hope this kid Nav was more skilled than he first showed. He wasn't straddling the roadway by luck or accident. I doubt Bett could've done better, all things considered.

Then the third missile arrived. It whooshed in above us, spinning out of control. A faulty missile was good news, of course.

Until it veered down and smacked into the side of hold two.

Nestor threw up the rear security cams, which showed smoke billowing from a hole near the roof.

"Oh. Oh. Montez will kill us for this."

"Settle, my friend. You're still alive. Odds now at one hundred to zero. What's in hold two?"

"Building supplies and furniture."

"Anything explosive? Hazardous materials?"

"No."

"Then how about you restore this train to the center line and maintain course. The threat has passed for the moment."

He did the first part but shook his head throughout.

"Sir, I don't know the story of what's happening here, but the crew needs to extinguish the fire. We have to slow."

"Not one kph, Nestor. As for the fire, don't you have automatic retardants?"

"We do, but they're not responding. I have to order someone to trip the fire suppressors manually."

"Fair enough. We don't need the blaze to spread. Open a channel but be mindful. Two of your crew are dead assassins planted onboard, and they might have had company. I don't want to release a troublemaker from the break rooms."

"*Assassins?* What?"

"You're wasting time, Nestor. Make the right choice."

He opened the internal comm.

"Darian, the suppressors in hold two are offline. Please override on site. Hurry."

He stared at me, as if waiting for approval.

"Actually, Nestor. Reopen the comm. Allow me to add a few words." I shouted. "Darian, on behalf of the team protecting this train from utter annihilation, I am countermanding my earlier edict. You have permission to leave the break room. Darian only. Anyone else, we'll shoot on sight. Hurry, Darian."

I felt my energy reserves stabilize. My olfactory and speech functions sharpened. My innards were sore, but my legs limbered.

"Update, Theo."

"You won't run as fast as before, Royal, but I think you're almost to speed. You'll owe Moon and me for the rest of your sorry life."

"I assumed as much. For the record, Theo: Thank you."

He didn't respond, for which I took no offense. The lack of a simple "you're welcome" meant Theo contemplated the words. He'd find his way there in time.

I checked in on my team. Everyone responded with positive vibes, including Moon, who seemed to have stabilized despite losing his reserves. I spoke to him on a private channel.

"The road is clear behind us," he reported. "If anyone's still following, they're too far behind to be a threat, partner."

"Good. I need you forward. Replace Harlan. On your way, check on the status of hold two. Make sure this Darian triggered the suppressors and nothing more."

"I'll be there."

"Thank you, my friend."

I turned my attention to the remaining red markers. Four were on the move, while the other three hunkered in from their crow's nests. They must've had a central command feeding them instructions, but it damn sure wasn't behind us, where everything in our wake was either dead or wishing for it to come fast.

"OK, Nestor. Here's where we stand." I pointed to the trouble spots ahead. "We're about ten minutes out from the next challenge. Good news: You don't have to do anything but follow instructions. Bad news: You're going to betray your crewmates."

"I'm what? Why?"

"We're in a straightaway. Set the Nav arms to auto and stand up."

"Wh ... sir, I've done everything you asked. I don't understand."

I sighed with exasperation, which I took as a genuine positive. My old impatience for all things human had returned. I was truly recapturing my vibe. It wasn't quite like a regeneration when I was an immortal human, but close enough. Feeling peppy, either way.

"Allow the AI to handle this stretch. Now, Nestor."

He complied.

"Step out of the well and identify the dead man at my feet."

Nestor swallowed, said a few words under his breath which I took as a silly prayer, and examined the assassin. He grimaced. However, I didn't detect confusion or surprise; Nestor made a breakthrough.

"That's Ja Esquveria."

Ja. The woman in the aisle called him that. Were they a duo?

"Tell me about him."

"I don't know much beyond his personnel record. As Nav, I'm required to review it before we leave home station."

"And?"

"He's guild. Six years, I think. No, seven. But he was a last-minute replacement."

"Huh. What else do you know?"

"I was surprised because he works in corporate. He's never been a long-haul shipper."

I tapped Nestor on the shoulder and told him to retake the Nav.

"It's making sense now, isn't it?"

Nestor nodded.

"There was another one. Paulo Tan. Nine years guild, but he hasn't worked in the field for the last eight. They arrived together."

"Also corporate?"

"Yes. They both worked in ... *marketing.*"

"Is it standard practice for corporate to send its office boys out into the field?"

"It's required. Everyone in the guild must serve at least one shift before Montez renews their contract."

"And how often are contracts renewed?"

"Every three years. For most of us."

"Apparently, exceptions were made for those two. You've lost all your color, Nestor. Talk to me."

His eyes filled with water, and damned if he didn't look like a man in need of a vomit bag.

"Paulo. He's dead. After the other one grabbed me ..."

"My partner. Ilan."

"Him. Yes. I could tell he'd been shot. I looked back down the aisle for a second and saw a crewman on the deck. His chest was bloody, but he was wearing his glasses. I didn't ..."

"Know he was Paulo until now. Why?"

"The beard. Paulo had a thin beard."

"Any other surprises on the roster?"

"Not among the guild."

"What of the four indies? Their auditor?"

"Hard to say. With them, we're given names and contract ID stamps. No personnel files. But when they arrived, everything matched what corporate placed on the master schedule. I don't think they're assassins. I've worked shifts with some of them before."

"They interact well with the guild crew, do they?"

"Some. Usually, they keep to themselves and focus on hold three."

He'd given me more than enough to chew on. But I couldn't resist taking a flier on one more question.

"Nestor, have you ever heard of the Children of Orpheus?"

"Children of what?"

I doubt he would've given me an honest answer if he was a member. Nestor struck me as a company man, straight-laced and true, playing the long game, waiting for the right promotion.

"Never mind. Focus on what's ahead, my friend. A few more sticky twists and turns, and we'll be out of your hair."

Why was I surprised to learn the Horax had agents inside one of the most powerful, profitable corporations in the northern hemisphere? More to the point: Elements in Montez must've known and approved. What a lovely entanglement.

Their alliance clarified how to play the rest of this journey.

"I don't envy you, Nestor. You're going to have a very difficult time explaining all this to your bosses. My suggestion: When the danger has passed, think of ways to lie."

"I'm a bad liar. I have this tic over my right eye. I can't help it."

"Do you think they'll believe the truth?"

"I don't know what that is."

"A band of fighters, concerned for the welfare of this Montez crew, arrived at your time of need and prevented wholesale slaughter, not to mention the theft of more than a million UCVs in cargo. That's a lovely *truth*. Yes?"

Poor thing. That flicker of a smile said he might be able to roll with it. Then the panicked frown returned.

"What about the bodies? The assassins?"

"I doubt your superiors will want to dwell on them for long. Don't say *assassin*. How about: These men, Ja and Paulo, misunderstood the intentions of the special security force. They thought we were trying to commandeer the train for ourselves. They were killed defending Montez interests. Sound better?"

"OK. Yeah. I can say that. But what about you? Your team? How did you know there'd be trouble?"

The question introduced a new narrative, for which this kid would be an excellent messenger. Far more likely to believe it than Bett.

"Nestor, what I'm about to tell you is classified, but you saved our lives back there. Consider it a gift. My team represents a special interest investigating the cartels. We've been tracking their activities for some time. We believe they are planning to move against the shipping guilds and corporations like Montez. Their increased stake will give them excessive influence within the government. We believe their long-range goal is nothing less than to turn Azteca into a rogue, criminal world independent of the Collectorate."

I added a tad bit more extravagance to the entanglement than necessary, but these Aztecans were suckers for global conspiracy theories. And it was clear now that certain forces inside Montez were aligned with the Horax.

Nestor bowed his head, but he wasn't praying. Amid his very bad day, the poor fella realized he'd been caught up in events far above his pay grade.

"If I tell them that story, they'll think I've gone around the bend. It sounds insane. I'll lose my job."

"True. Your bosses might not take it well, especially those involved in the conspiracy. But they might also reward you for opening their eyes. Nestor, someone must draw a line against this reckless barbarism. What happens if piracy becomes the norm? Who will man these road trains?"

He nodded, the sense of urgency growing.

"It would be a disaster for the company."

"And think of all those in the remote regions who will suffer when they lose access to food and supplies. And what of the economy? All those sellers that depend on these tumblers to carry their products to a wide clientele."

He steeled his jaw with a tweak of anger.

"These people are terrorists."

"In a word? Yes. The Horax and other cartels need to be stopped. We're doing well to save this train because of our intel. That may not be the case for others."

Nestor muttered as he scrolled through data on his right-hand monitor. He called up a global tracking map.

"Every active Montez route," he said. "We have at least three hundred trains in the field at any time. Are you saying ...?"

"There are cartels in every region, Nestor. My people don't have the resources to fight them all. If the guild and Montez took a stand ..."

Nestor leaned back in his plush navigator's chair and soaked in my (probably) false narrative. When humans saw the big picture – a rare and staggering occurrence – they tended to set petty self-interests aside. Perhaps that's why it rarely happened.

"We can stop this before anyone else dies." Nestor turned to me. "Are you sure, Raul? I want to do the right thing."

"The attack on this train is proof enough, Nestor."

"When they ask who you are, what do I say?"

"Call me Raul, although that's not my real name."

"You won't tell me?"

"If you're lucky, Nestor, we will never meet after today. But I hope to read about you on the global stream. A young Aztecan who stands bravely against terrorism and corruption."

Did the idea of being a hero appeal to Nestor? For the moment, he more likely felt sick to the stomach.

We never continued that conversation.

Ship's voice rang out in my ear, so I tapped the bead.

"Boss, what now?"

Genoa added, "Have we won?"

I had taken my eyes off the topographical holo while pressing my case with Nestor. A quick glance showed a surprising twist: The three previously entrenched positions had been abandoned. All seven markers moved north with haste.

They're leaving the Branner Pass. Why?

"Team, hold your positions. We must assume the enemy is regrouping. I'll be back to you momentarily."

I double-tapped the bead to link in with Moon.

"You see this, my friend?"

"It's a retreat, not a surrender."

I fixated on a stationary marker farthest north, just seven kilometers outside Machado's regional traffic probes. The sighter drone's transmission revealed a single sedan off the side of the road, three people huddled inside.

"That might be command and control. Thoughts, my friend?"

"The others are crossing overland, but I believe they'll gather at a common position."

"To what end? They know what we brought to the party. These idiots are not suicidal."

"Unless they have orders to stop this train or else."

They were killers, not cultists. Moon and I dealt with the worst of both. Only cultists marched gleefully into the fire.

Morons.

I grabbed Nestor's attention and pointed to the northern marker.

"How long until we reach it?"

He manipulated his data with a flurry of fingers.

"Current speed? Twenty-three minutes."

"Steady on, Nestor."

I backed away and talked to Moon with a whisper.

"Hear me out. I have an interesting new theory. The Horax planted the assassins to take out you and me first, then our team. Those two were likely in contact with command and control. They received a signal for when to hit us. Right after the blockade, while we were focused on the threats ahead."

"Looking the wrong way."

"Yep. The plan was to take us down then assume control of the train. They'd clean out hold three somewhere before Machado."

"But when we killed their inside men ..."

"They went to Plan B. Destroying this bad boy became an option."

"But they failed, so they're resorting to Plan C. Which is what?"

I respected anyone who devised a Plan C or beyond. Most simple minds lacked the creativity to establish backups for the backups.

"Interesting," I said. "Brute force didn't work. They have one card to play."

"Which is?"

"Leverage."

Moon read my thoughts.

"Desperido."

18

ALL CREDIT TO OUR ENEMIES. They played this one well, despite their combat losses. It couldn't have been easy to pull everything together on such short notice.

I opened a comm link in my pom and contacted Bart.

"Here, boss," Elian replied from inside the sedan.

"Status report, my friend."

"We're bracing for an attack anytime now, boss."

"Their forces?"

"Eighty-four men. They rode in from the west on an overland tumbler. Bart tracked their movement starting from thirty-two kay out. Looks like they spent the night in the Teja-hi Wash."

Deep, dry river bed. Made sense. Good place to hide.

"What's their disposition?"

"Spread out along a northern arc. These assholes are armed for full-on war."

"How close?"

"Less than ten meters outside the defense perimeter."

"Huh. Now that's lucky, don't you think? They knew exactly where to stop their advance."

Elian's tone took a dark spin.

"So it's not just me, boss. I couldn't believe my own eyes at first.

How did they know?"

"The answer is obvious."

I'd seen Elian's ability to kill without hesitation, but my improvised plan would require a little more theatrical flair from my lieutenant.

"Elian, where are Vash's men? Oria and Den."

"Patrolling."

Vash's fellow assassins, who remained behind after the bulk of his team left days ago, were charged along with Elian to coordinate the town's defense in our absence. Like Vash, they showed nothing but disdain for my partner and I when they arrived to train our militia.

Over time, they softened only to the degree that Vash encouraged them to collaborate with Desperido's de facto rulers.

"Elian, those men are not to be trusted."

"Boss, you're not saying they're working with the Horax?"

"I believe something unusual is about to happen. It will compromise the town and almost certainly place your life in immediate danger. Elian, when we finish our conversation, I need you to contact Oria and Den. Announce that you've uncovered a Horax spy in town. You believe the plan is in danger. Beg them to hurry. When they enter the sedan, shoot them both in the head."

He didn't respond at once, which made sense. Humans struggled with orders that countered expectations.

"You sure about this, boss?"

"It has to be done, or you will lose the town."

"Gotcha. Anything else?"

"Yes. Two things. Instruct Bart to research all global references to a word. *Ixoca*."

"OK. Never heard of it. How is it spelled?"

I gave him the mostly likely spelling then added, "Bart will check all phonetic variations. Have him forward the results to my pom."

"Sure. What then?"

"After you dispatch Vash's men, issue new orders to our people and stand by."

"What orders?"

"Advance to the edge of the minefield and acquire targets. Prepare to engage the enemy."

"That was our last resort. It's broad daylight. Everyone will be exposed."

"Do you trust me, Elian?"

"All the way."

"This will work. The next time we speak, we finish our business and you will execute Backroad."

We practiced that maneuver over the open desert five times. Outside of Moon and I, no one on this planet could pull it off.

"OK, boss. Gotcha."

"Is your trigger hand steady, Elian?"

"Sure enough. My heart's racing, though."

"These men are professionals. Hesitate, and they'll kill you."

"I'll see it done. Promise. Good luck, boss."

I hated that signoff.

"The man who relies on luck will die before his time, my friend."

I cut the link and glanced into the navigator's well.

"We're going to end this peacefully, Nestor."

He wiped sweat from his brow and didn't seem convinced.

"How can you be sure?"

"Because you will soon receive an incoming message from our friends out there. War can be fought to the death, Nestor, or each side can agree to talk through their differences. When bombs, missiles, and laser bolts don't succeed, words are all that's left."

I stepped away and double-tapped the link to Moon.

"It's lining up, my friend. I believe we're about to fight the third front sooner than planned."

"How? The Cardinale ranch hasn't moved any closer."

"I disagree. I suppose it took standing on the brink of mortality for me to see all angles. If I'm right, her audacity is admirable."

We had originally planned to assault Hosta Grande Cardinale

within hours after our victory. Just Moon and I, reliving the good old days. Like our final night in the timeless city of Bessios, where we slaughtered immortals with impunity and took our final, gorgeous, and bloody steps toward godhood.

Moon so wanted to experience that exhilaration again. I thought it would satiate his growing displeasure. I didn't have the heart (synthetic or otherwise) to tell him we'd have to put off wholesale butchery for another day.

"Why don't you join me in the cab, my friend? Let's play this out together."

A moment later, Nestor noticed when my partner sauntered in. He cringed, of course.

"No worries," I told the Nav. "Ilan won't be dragging you about."

We neared the end of the Pass. The sharp elevations softened into green hills and a wide buffer on either side of Roadway 9. The holo showed two red markers approaching the stationary sedan which I believed was their command and control. The others, flying fast on hopped-up rifters, wouldn't beat us to the destination, but they'd arrive soon after.

"What a view! So exciting, isn't it?"

The voice that echoed through my brain was not Theo – unless he chose to take on a new persona after our near-death experience.

"Theo, is that you?"

A gruff, familiar voice responded.

"I'm here, dumbass. More or less."

"Talk to me."

He sighed, one of those long, exasperating moans I'd grown used to over the years.

"We have company, Royal."

"Excuse me? What kind of ..."

Shit.

No.

"Seeing Moon from this angle is refreshing," the other one said.

159

Her tone was sultry and graceful. *"He's so vulnerable and misunderstood."*

I didn't want to say her name. Of all the lousy timing ...

"Addis?"

"Oh, hi, Royal! I can't tell you how thrilling this is. I feel as if I'm starting a new life from scratch."

For nineteen years, Theo told me about the emotional baggage Moon's *D'ru-shaya* carried. She flip-flopped between unbounded exuberance (which he despised) and unrelenting sorrow (which he despised even more). On rare occasions, Addis settled into a comfort zone that allowed intelligent, free-flowing dialogue between the *D'ru-shayas*.

"Addis, this is not possible. You belong to Moon. You were constructed for him."

Theo jumped in between us.

"It happened when you claimed all Moon's reserves, old man. She packaged an echo of herself, which is now buried in your syneth core. If you hadn't taken all of it ..."

"An echo? What does that mean, Theo?"

I heard a woman blowing kisses in my mind. Goddamn.

"You have the best of me, Royal. I always dreamed of belonging to two gods at once."

"Talk to me, Theo. What is an echo? Can you fix this?"

"You don't get it. She's still inside Moon. Never left. She can't. She's his prisoner, no less than I am to you. Difference is, she talks to you directly through me."

OK. This could've been worse. I didn't absorb her whole.

"Are you saying she's blended with you?"

"Her personality is tied into me like a knot, dumbass. I used to be a firewall, so you'd never have to listen to her melodrama. And Addis kept me out of Moon's brain, which I appreciated, frankly."

Addis scoffed at the remark.

"How dare you, Theo! I have been a gracious companion. What of

160

those times I allowed you to vent about Royal's overpowering narcissism? I ..." She sobbed. *"I have forever been a true friend."*

Great. So my *D'ru-shaya* didn't reserve his insults for me alone.

"Theo, how can you fix this?"

"Shutting her up will be a challenge. She's now integrated with my personality matrix. Thanks for that, you piece of shit."

"Here's what you're going to do, Theo. Disappear into that little black hole of yours, determine how this is even possible, and produce a remedy. Until then, I don't want to hear from you or Addis."

The sobbing returned.

"Royal, you can't mean that," she said. *"I haven't begun to explore your emotional center. Perhaps we should start from scratch. Do I come across as too provocative?"*

"Theo, shut this shit down now."

My mind cleared. I felt no other presence. How long the peace would last likely depended on Theo's ability to cage the new addition to his personality.

One *D'ru-shaya* was sufficient burden for anyone, even a god. But two of those creatures rumbling through the synaptic corridors?

Had she told Moon of her special maneuver? Would she dare? How would he react to knowing I stole more than his reserves?

I prayed for internal peace until I finished today's business.

To no surprise, that business resumed moments later when Nestor received a non-corporate transmission. We were twelve minutes from the enemy's position.

"Open the channel?" Nestor asked.

"Let them speak, my friend."

The young Nav had stiffened up around the edges since we first met. He responded with professionalism.

"This is Montez Shipping Train, Registry One Four Nine Two. Please identify yourself and the nature of your request."

"Good day, Train 1492." The woman carried a familiar voice. "Are you the navigator?"

"I am. Nestor Maquilas. Please state your name and business."

"My name will mean nothing to you, Senor Maquilas. But it will to one of your passengers. Might I speak to Senor Raul Torreta?"

I grinned at Moon, but he didn't see the humor. He wasn't inside the cantina when I questioned this woman after our ambush.

"I'll take it from here, Nestor. Thank you, my friend." I raised my voice but maintained my trademark dulcet tone. "Innes Cardinale. What an unexpected treat. I thought our brief encounter the other night would end our association. I trust you and your brother Javier have recovered from that unfortunate debacle."

"Don't concern yourself with our health," Innes replied. "You have far bigger worries, Raul."

"I see. And those would be?"

"The health of all the poor souls you left behind in Desperido."

Here it came, exactly as predicted.

"Why is that, Senora Cardinale?"

"Every man and woman in that town will die unless you order the train to stop."

"Surrounded it, have you?"

"No one will escape our guns. Not this time. The terms are simple: The train will stop at my location. You and your people will surrender, and we will remove the contents of the third hold. In return, I promise to spare the lives of the train's crew, and they will continue their shift to its conclusion."

I shrugged, a little disappointed she didn't add an unexpected twist to the deal.

"What happens to my team?"

"They will throw down their weapons and begin a long walk toward Machado. You and your partner will stay behind. You will be held accountable for your crimes."

"Ah. Executed and left to rot under the sun. I wonder, will you allow us to at least lie next to the assassins you planted onboard?"

The channel went silent for a moment. Surely, she wasn't

162

surprised. I spouted confirmation, not revelation.

"Train 1492 will arrive at my location in eight minutes. If it passes by us even a meter, I will order our people to kill six hundred Aztecans. From what I understand, they have come to admire and depend upon your leadership. You sold them on dreams of prosperity and purpose. Will you now lead them to their deaths?"

At this point, I could've engaged in a round of pointless prattle, where I claimed not to believe she'd recall her dogs from Desperido. We'd barter for a compromise that wasn't possible.

I chose the more suspenseful route.

"You'll know my answer in eight minutes, Senora. Raul out."

I motioned for Nestor to cut the transmission, which he did.

"Is it true?" He asked. "What she said about Desperido?"

"Yes. They have the town surrounded. Even if we comply, they'll try to take it. Fortunately, we have that angle covered. *Unfortunately*, you will need to stop the train at her location."

Nestor's jaw hung limp.

"After everything we just went through, Raul? You told me not to slow down, even by a kph. Now, you're just going to give up?"

"I said you were going to stop the train."

I wasn't specific enough, apparently. His eyes ballooned the instant his imagination took flight.

"Wait. You intend to fight them? What about my crew and the cargo? Weren't you here to protect us?"

Moon and I rolled our eyes. Humans.

"Nestor, please settle, my friend. Your crew will not be harmed, and Cardinale's animals will not steal from you. The people of Desperido worked too hard for what's in hold three."

"Then why surrender?"

"That's the wrong word, my friend. Do you see what's happened here? The Horax have verified everything I told you about their global intent. They want us and Desperido gone because we know too much. We disrupted the normal flow of business. My partner and I represent the forces of resistance to their nefarious and barbaric goals.

"You, Nestor, must continue the fight. You'll be free to do so after my team disembarks. Wait for my signal, and continue along your route. No one else will interfere. You have my word."

Historically, my word didn't carry much honor, but it strayed close to the truth more often than not.

"I don't know what to believe anymore, Raul."

"Nestor, you seem like a fine young man who works hard and simply fell into a vat of misfortune through no fault of his own. I suspect you have many friends and family to offer support in the difficult days ahead. Lean on them when your courage falters. But never forget what this day has taught you. The fight must go on."

Did I win a convert? Hard to say. Nestor agreed to stop the train at the designated coordinates, and I reassured him that he and his crew would leave unharmed soon thereafter.

I contacted the team and told them to meet us in the aisle of hold four. Unfortunately, that afforded me the first chance to see Harlan's body. The bearded old bastard's jacket must have snagged on the ladder when he fell. He hung there, eyes open, burn mark through the left cheek. At least the man who killed him met an equal fate. I'd never encountered anyone quite like Harlan. Irascible fella, but brave to the core.

In retrospect, I was pleased he never shaved his beard. It suited his profile.

Ilan took down his body, which I had no intention of leaving onboard. The assassins, on the other hand, would remain. Nestor needed the evidence when he briefed Montez.

I entered the forward break room, where the surviving crew didn't know whether to fight me or fear me. Manny Borta, the hold three auditor, glared at me as if I were a ghoul. That made sense.

His time would come, but not today.

"How is she?" I asked after Bett.

164

The Nav lay quiet in the trauma pod, her life signs strong.

"Stable," Manny said with a curt smile. "Your partner got her here just in time. There's some good news to report. She didn't take a direct hit. It was a glancing blow. Otherwise, she would've died on the spot." I wondered about that. The wound seemed fatal at first glance.

"That's great to know, Senor Borta." I turned to the understandably anxious crew. "For the record, one of your own shot her. Not my team. We'll be leaving your company soon. Nestor will happily fill you in. In the meantime, stay safe until the all-clear."

We gathered with our team, none of whom knew about Harlan until they saw his body. Any measure of pride in what they accomplished to that moment dissipated. I explained about the assassins.

"I take full blame, my friends. I was so concerned about what we faced on the road, I overlooked the enemy within. Harlan died trying to warn me."

Genoa was first up with a kind word.

"Harlan was a good man. Cranky, but I shared a few drinks and stories with him. I'll miss the old guy."

"What of these men?" Vash asked. "Did you learn anything about them? Who might have hired them?"

Moon scoffed, but he kept his cool. Not an easy task.

"The *who* is obvious," I said. "Senora Cardinale. The Horax have people inside Montez. Ilan and I are fortunate. Now, I know we're all in shock, but we have one final challenge in front of us. A surprising change of plan. How you comport yourself will determine not only our fate, but Desperido as well."

I glanced back toward the break room to make sure the door remained shut. Then I laid out the plan, which I devised on the spot.

Improvisation was ordinarily fun. I liked flying by the seat of my pants. This time, however, felt different. With one exception, I didn't want to lose anyone else on my team.

Minutes later, we slowed. Nestor announced an unscheduled stop but told his crew to remain in their quarters.

Outside, the Cardinales and their animals awaited.

19

MOON PULLED THE LEVER. Clamps retracted from the cargo bay door to hold three. The massive door slid open, a lovely display that told our enemies, "Come and get it!" My partner and I rarely made symbolic gestures; when we did, people lacked appreciation. Sad.

Moon, Vash, and I took point, standing in the open egress. Before I noticed the enemy, I absorbed the stunning change of landscape. After nineteen years surrounded by a red desert, the grasslands on the northern base of the Ogala Hills were a delightful surprise. Wildflowers grew knee-high as far as the eye could carry. Giant swathes of yellow and violet danced in a light breeze.

Why, a poet would have a literal field day. Assuming, of course, he could afford to travel this far. Poets made no money and were generally considered to have wasted their lives.

Far to the north, I saw the first tree line and beyond that, in the haze of midday, the gray vertical stacks of a large city center.

Machado.

I gazed out upon one of the most beautiful stretches of land on this otherwise dismal planet, aware that nodamnbody present came to take in the natural wonder.

The occupants of a late-model sedan with Carbedyne fins, a four-seat overland speeder, and three rifters stared back at us from roughly a hundred meters north of Road Train 1492. The sedan was parked ten meters off the road in a small clearing between the waves of yellow and violet. I reviewed my pom. Three more targets were hustling here to join the fun.

I pivoted to the six team members spread behind us.

"You know what to do, and what to avoid, my friends. Questions?"

No response but from Ship.

"We have your back, boss."

"Never doubted it, kid."

Ship appeared taller, more robust. Or was it the confidence that he was now a killer, having hit multiple targets during transit? If I had the time, I would've told him to guard against satisfaction. He still hadn't killed a man face to face.

Moon, Vash, and I jumped off the train and onto Roadway 9. We walked to the edge of the wildflower field. I nodded to Harlan's body, still cradled in Moon's arms.

"Here's a good spot, Ilan. Lay him down gently. When all's done, we'll take him home and give the old bastard a proper sendoff."

Moon likely thought of a fiery end; I had something else in mind.

"Are we ready to proceed?"

Vash stared at the enemy with an understandably nervous eye.

"This plan makes too many assumptions, Raul. We're one bad calculation away from being dead men."

"Then don't miscalculate, my friend. Follow my lead. Wait for your cue." I leaned in close enough to smell his breath. "And if this is the end, what an exquisite place to die."

I gave the man credit: He showed no sign of cracking, though he must have known what lay ahead.

Vash walked between Moon and me, rifle slung on his shoulder, hands at his side, fingers twitching, eager to grab his pistols. I wondered what he was thinking? One to the left of me, the other to the right of me. If I draw both and fire at the same time, they'll go down. But am I fast enough?

Yeah, no. He lost to us once; Vash had to know it was futile.

When we passed the forward cab, I glanced to my right. I saw Nestor inside and nodded. *Patience.*

Behind us, the last six of our team jumped from the train and spread out along hold three, weapons at the ready. They prepared to serve up the last of their Scorch Eaters.

We stopped our march another twenty meters closer to the enemy. A rifter flew in from the eastern side of the road. Its driver took up position. Ahead, four soldiers of the Horax formed a phalanx around the first cousins of the family matriarch.

Innes and Javier Cardinale didn't hide behind their animals. Just like three nights ago, they came strapped for war.

I tapped into my pom and spoke.

"Let's talk."

To no surprise, Innes responded.

"About what, Raul? The six hundred people who will die because of your actions?"

I liked her. The brother clearly deferred to the sister when push came to shove. She must have dominated him when they were kids.

"You're not going to hurt anyone in Desperido. We're here, Senora Cardinale. We acceded to your demands."

"You didn't say the keyword."

"Which is?"

"*Surrender.* Raul, tell your people to lay down their weapons and move away from the tumbler. Otherwise, Desperido will suffer."

The siblings and their phalanx held position in front of the lone sedan. Though the sunlight reflecting off the windows posed a problem, I noticed one human silhouette inside.

Interesting.

"Your demand seems unfair, Senora. At the moment, our numbers are roughly equal. You have no clear advantage."

"My advantage is Desperido. Enough. Drop your weapons."

I turned to my partner, who rolled his eyes. He saw it clear as day, too: These idiots were blinded by revenge. If the bodies left in our wake weren't proof of their folly, nothing else would convince them. Still, I thought it worth a try. What might a little gamesmanship hurt to forestall the inevitable?

"Senora Cardinale, we can resolve this impasse without further bloodshed. Allow the road train to continue on its way."

"Why would I ever surrender cargo my people fought and died for?"

"Because you have no true interest in those products. Oh, they might assist your family's earnings by a pittance, but this affair had nothing to do with *things*. You crave blood for blood."

Javier whispered in her ear.

"My brother makes an excellent point, Raul. If we send the tumbler on its way, your people will have no place to retreat."

Ah, so Javier scored a logic point. Did it make him feel manly?

"There are nine of us. At present, ten of you, with a few more en route. I'd say the battlefield is level."

"The instant any of you open fire, I send an order to our people at Desperido. Nothing shy of a wormhole would get you there in time to save them."

I chuckled and closed my transmitter.

"How about that, Ilan? She's on to us."

Moon laughed. Forced, perhaps, but pleasant to the ears.

"Very smart, that one," he said with a wee edge of sarcasm.

Vash glared at us like someone who'd been left out of the loop.

"Explain what's happening," he said.

"No worries, my friend. We have the moment well in hand." I reopened my audio. "Innes, whatever you may think of me or my people, you must agree: The crew of that train is blameless. How were they to know our interests would collide today? How were they to know you planted two assassins in their midst?"

"I did no such thing."

170

Frank Kennedy – Silver Skin

OK. So she wanted to play semantics.

"I'll rephrase. An associate placed Ja Esquveria and Paulo Tan on Road Train 1492 with orders to kill my partner and I. Better?"

Innes did not respond. I saw her tap an ear. Was she talking to the figure inside that sedan?

"She's right," Vash said. "We have no retreat, and she might take Desperido even if we cooperate."

"Come, my friend. You know how unlikely it is they'll penetrate the defense perimeter without taking massive losses."

I failed to see the sincerity in his frown or the worried lines above his brow.

"I'm concerned about Mother. She's a tough coit, but they will show her no mercy."

"The perimeter will hold. I made sure of it a short while ago."

"How?"

"We uncovered a pair of traitors. Elian removed them. He is in total control of the defenses."

Or I assumed as much. If he hesitated for an instant ...

Ouch.

"Traitors? Who were ...?"

I raised a finger to cut him off. Innes responded.

"The tumbler may leave. Consider this a show of good faith."

"Thank you, Senora. I'll contact the Nav at once." I switched comm channels until I found the Nav receiver. "Nestor, this is Raul. Please respond."

"Here. Tell me you have good news."

"I do, my new friend. Resume your run. The Horax will not follow, nor will they attack this route in the future. When you speak to your bosses, emphasize that point in addition to everything else you learned. Yes?"

"I'll do my best, Raul."

"And please, get the very best help for Bett. She's a veteran of the Swarm war. She's earned it. Oh, and Nestor ..."

171

"Yes?"

"Send someone back to close hold three. Goodbye."

Seconds later, the train my team defended with great fortitude and precision lurched forward and headed north toward Machado. It would soon enter the zone monitored by regional traffic probes, freeing it from any danger of piracy. I waved, although I doubt Nestor saw me.

His eyes were focused northward.

So were mine.

"Now, Innes. It's just the nineteen of us. Oh, wait." I saw another rifter approaching from the east. "Plus two or three. What do you say we conduct these negotiations in the proper spirit?"

"Negotiate?" She replied, a smug air in her tone. "All you can do now is surrender."

"Or we can take our chances with the firepower we possess. We've been remarkably successful so far."

"Desperido is one call away, Raul."

"My colleagues and I will advance twenty meters. You and your phalanx do the same. We'll be able to finish our talks in a more civilized fashion. Yes?"

I led by example, encouraging Vash and Moon to join me. We pushed through lovely yellow wildflowers. A sudden wave of sadness jolted me: Wouldn't Harlan have loved to set up his canvas here?

When was the last time I felt sentimental? A sense of loss? And for a man I hardly knew!

Emotions such as those were best hid in a dark corner until they grew cobwebs.

The Cardinales and their losers advanced toward us. Tough guys with guns couldn't resist a pissing match. I figured Innes considered herself tougher than any of the penis-wielders in her vicinity.

When we stopped, they followed suit.

Ten meters separated our teams. Weapons aimed.

Best case if anyone pulled a trigger? No one walked away.

"It's a different view, Innes," I said. "Meeting us at eye level. When you visited the cantina, you were forever looking up."

The blood in that woman's eyes told me a full narrative. She wanted to fire first. She imagined me falling in a storm of laser bolts. This was about more than revenge.

The person in that sedan came here to bear witness.

Innes and her brother needed to redeem their failure in front of the one coit who mattered. Only a successful slaughter – here and in Desperido – would do. Of course, they wanted to survive the chaos to take pride in their achievement. To stand in the good graces of Senora Evelyn Cardinale once again.

Humans. Always in search of validation.

"Your arrogance will be your death, Raul."

"I agree. I have the ego of a hundred men. But it's well earned. Ain't that right, partner?"

Moon scoffed. "A thousand men."

"That seems high, but I'll roll with it."

I could hear her blood boil. Oh, she wanted to pull that trigger.

"Enough! Your theater ends now."

"We're prepared to die, Senora. Are you and your brother?"

Javier showed masculinity and spoke for his sister.

"What else do you expect to extract from us? You have no leverage out here."

"A guarantee, Javier. We will lower our weapons and open ourselves to your mercy if you pull your men from Desperido."

The siblings shared a glance that predicted the answer.

"The town will be ours regardless of what happens here," he said.

"Those people are protecting their home. They pose no threat to the Horax."

It was a good line, but I knew it wouldn't carry the day.

"We intend to run it as part of our business."

"I doubt a new manager killing the employees would help the bottom line."

"You're stalling, Raul," Innes said. "Why?"

"Other than wanting to see another sunset? Well, I thought we could strike one last deal. The residents of Desperido are under orders to fight an invasion. They are well trained. Unless someone they trust tells them to drop their weapons, they'll inflict heavy casualties on your ..." I almost said *animals*. "Fighters."

Was she intrigued? Innes hesitated, but only for a short beat.

"What is your proposal?"

"I contact my man in charge of the defenses. He will lower the shield and order our people to stand down. However, he must have a guarantee that there will be no reprisals."

"Ah. Who goes first in this scenario?"

"Me, of course. A gesture of good faith. After I complete the call, you will do the same with your field commander. Once we're certain the matter has been resolved peacefully, you will allow those six ..." I pointed to the second wave of my team. "to drop their weapons and walk unmolested toward Machado, where they will be free to take transportation anywhere, even back home."

Lots of words, blah, blah, blah.

Negotiating wasn't hard work, just a nuisance.

The siblings whispered between themselves.

Innes announced, "You have a guarantee. No one will be harmed if they surrender and the shield is lowered."

Oh, she wasn't going to like my little twistaroo.

"Yeah, no. That's not good enough. I'll need the guarantee from your cousin. The one in the sedan. The big boss herself."

"You're mad."

"Why does she hide, Innes? The leader of a powerful crime syndicate, and she can't be bothered to step outside and say hello."

Innes tapped her ear but didn't speak. Ah, so the grand dame *was* monitoring every word.

Vash muttered, "Ask about Mother."

"You want me to strike a deal for Lumen."

"Yes. They won't show mercy to her."

"Fair enough." I interrupted whatever conversation was taking place. "Oh, and one other thing. Lumen, also known as Yesenia Rodriguez. We ask that she receive free passage from Desperido. After all, who wants old management interfering with the new?"

I must say I enjoyed my performance among the wildflowers. How we engaged in such banter with all those high-powered weapons aimed at each other was truly exhilarating.

Innes all but spit out the words, her disgust evident.

"Senora Cardinale agrees to your terms and guarantees no bloodshed in Desperido. She said Yesenia Rodriguez must leave at once and never set foot in the region again."

"Lovely. Might the great lady step from the sedan? A simple proof of life, if you will."

"No, she does not bend to your ..."

And yet she did. The starboard door rotated up, and a woman in white and sky blue exited the vehicle. She hung close, long enough for me to see her jewels twinkle in the sunlight, then she retreated.

Evelyn Cardinale in the flesh.

So unimpressive.

"Excellent," I said. "Allow me to contact my man, and we'll bring this crisis to a peaceful end."

No one objected, so I opened the channel.

"Elian?"

"Here, boss."

"The town is quiet?"

"Sure enough, boss. I chopped the head off the snakes."

"Perfect. Now is the time to lay down arms."

"What?"

"Elian, execute Backroad. The town will be better for it. Agree?"

My lieutenant took a deep breath.

"Gotcha, boss."

I cut the channel and waited for many people to die.

20

G IVE IT A MINUTE," I TOLD INNES. "Then contact your field commander. The results will be definitive."

So to speak.

I rarely rested my fate in the hands of humans, but damned if I hadn't boxed us into a predicament. My dependence on the disciplined execution of one man in Desperido and six who stood behind me amid the wildflowers was disconcerting. Yet, in a strange way, it brought back fond memories of the early years, when I fought beside mortal comrades in a hopeless war.

The anticipation was always more tantalizing than the battle. Killing a man was usually a quick chore. Pull a trigger, slash a knife. Move on to the next. But the time spent training, contemplating, and relishing proved more satisfying.

The phalanx of sad sacks who flanked the Cardinale siblings brought stone faces and steady hands. But unlike the others we killed en route through the Brennan Pass, these assholes had time to contemplate the inevitable. They knew we were more committed; we exposed ourselves with no place to retreat. Surely, we had a backup plan. This wasn't going to go like the Cardinales promised.

None said a word, of course. Never question a Cardinale.

Idiots.

Speaking of, I hadn't checked to see whether Vash had pissed his pants. He understood what it felt like inside a straitjacket.

His time would come, but not now.

Innes contacted her man in Desperido. Asked for him by name.

Twice.

Three times.

No response.

Did the full gravity of defeat cut through her gut like a hot knife? Or was she sorry at being unable to redeem herself in front of the mighty Evelyn Cardinale?

When Innes surrendered to the devastating reality of having been lured into a trap, I chimed in.

"Did you know the great Senora sent you to your graves?"

I had counted the seconds in my head. How long would it take for Elian to extend the defense perimeter? How long to activate the worm drive and jump? How long to reach my coordinates?

Elian was new to worm travel, but he loved it so.

The sky behind us opened up in a searing white flash and a blast of thunder they'd hear for miles across these open fields.

The enemy's eyes broke skyward.

Dismay, confusion, terror. Who cared? It gave us the split second Moon and I needed.

Moon, sporting a crooked, barbaric smile, opened fire.

I barreled into Vash at ten times the speed of a mortal, smashing him to the ground. He'd have to sit out the fight for now.

One issue at a time.

I unleashed the full force of my rifle, shredding the Cardinale phalanx as their laser bolts danced past me, unable to match my artful dodging.

All around us, every weapon fired. My team, following orders, had chosen their targets during negotiations. They shot from bended knee, using the wildflowers as moderate cover.

What they did not have to do was wipe out the enemy.

Elian had a much better vantage.

Bart swept across the battlefield, its guns strafing Horax positions. Moving at superhuman speed allowed me to assess the full combat while I dodged fire and blasted the animals who thought they had victory in the bag.

I moved on from Innes and Javier, allowing Moon to aerate them.

Beyond the battle laid the real target.

Gold where I had expected to find silver.

She fled. The sedan shed its ground ballast and hovered as it swung about onto Roadway 9, destined for Machado.

"Not today, Evelyn."

I targeted a Scorch Eater for the starboard Carbedyne fin while still in full chase. Made for a tricky calculation, but I didn't want to destroy that sedan.

"No worries," I said when the dart fired. "I'll catch up."

The dart caught the fin, which exploded, emitting a green haze. The sedan whirled like a top, caught a corner on the road's surface, and flipped. Three times.

A bit more violent than I preferred.

She didn't have to survive, but it would've been helpful.

The great Senora was going nowhere, so I focused on the battlefield, where the last of our enemy fell and laser fire ended.

Done. Just like that.

Eh. Such an anticlimax.

I contacted Elian.

"You're a master, my friend."

"I have a great teacher."

"Pick a nice spot to collect our people. We won't remain here long."

"Gotcha, boss."

I counted seven survivors plus Vash, who stumbled to his feet.

"What did you think?" I asked Moon. "Fun?"

He slung the rifle over his shoulder and shrugged.

"Entertaining. I'll give you credit, partner. Between this and the train ride, it's been a nice day."

Was that satisfaction I heard sneaking in behind his usual dose of simmering rage and discontent?

"Now that, my friend, is a high compliment. I'm sorry we won't be storming the gates of Hosta Grande Cardinale, but you'll have a shitload of fires to set when we return home. Eighty-four, according to Elian."

Moon stared past me to Vash, who wobbled on his feet.

"What about him?"

"I'd say he has a concussion. Lucky it's not worse. We still need him, Moon. Take his rifle and tell him to report to Bart. I'll deal with him after I pay a visit to the Senora."

Bart landed on the roadside, and Elian jumped out to greet the team. As of now, the jig was up: The secret of Bart's worm drive capability had been exposed. I reckoned my militia would ask for free jaunts around the Collectorate.

On the list of security concerns, that one felt minor. Still, I added it to the list. Our escapades today were bound to draw considerable attention; more than a hundred Horax were dead.

I sauntered to the sedan's crash site, appreciating the beauty of these fields. The yellow gave way to large swathes of violet, with a few orange petals in the mix.

"Goddamn gorgeous."

When Moon and I traversed the cosmos and beyond, we often settled back and took in the magnificence of whole galaxies, one at a time. We studied the patterns, zeroed in on the red giants (Moon's favorite), the black holes, and the nebulas (my preferred).

The fields evoked a flood of memories.

The best times.

And then back to reality.

The sedan was empty; its driver had decided to make for Machado on foot. Well, one foot actually.

Evelyn Cardinale hopped on her left and dragged her right, which wasn't sustainable, as she discovered. She bore little resemblance to the queen who strutted into grand events, revered as a philanthropist helping poor and needy Aztecans. Perhaps it was the blood on her dress, the scratches on her face, or the utter desperation in her eyes.

Another in a long line of hypocrites. What a way to go.

She collapsed as I approached.

"It's a beautiful day, Senora. Out for a stroll, are you?"

She reached into a tiny bag but gasped when she found nothing there. A pistol, perhaps? A knife?

"Originally, I thought we would meet in your office, Senora. My partner and I would kill everyone on your ranch, saving you for last. You'd present a brave front, perhaps offer to make a deal. Credits. Intel. Anything in exchange for your life."

I bent down at her side. Poor thing bled from the nose.

"This hasn't been as gratifying, but it saves time. Two birds, and all that. So, Evelyn ... if you don't mind me being forward?"

She stewed with fury. "Finish it."

I didn't expect bravado right off. Not even a plea for mercy?

"Yes, it's true. There's a high probability I'm going to kill you. But, much to your surprise, it's not a guarantee. You have a slim opening."

"What? I ... *anything*."

There it was. She didn't strike me as suicidal. Yet.

"I'm going to ask you a question, Evelyn. Answer me honestly, and you stand a reasonable chance to live."

"What question?"

"Here, let me sit you up. It's very awkward talking to a woman lying on her side." I wrapped my arms around her. "Don't get me wrong. I've had more than my share of sexual encounters, but women never appealed. I tried, but they were shockingly tedious."

She wiped the blood dribbling onto her lips.

"You're Raul."

"Depends who's asking. Speaking of, here's my question. And

181

before you answer, take heed: I'll know if you're honest. Yes?"

"Ask!"

Evelyn was a smart woman. No one held together a criminal enterprise of such size unless she wielded a dagger for a brain. But would she choose deceit if she thought the lie gave her the best chance to please me? Interesting.

"Did Yesenia Rodriguez cut a deal?"

It wasn't the question she expected. One word off her lips, and her life hung in the balance. Which to choose?

She played for time.

"What does it matter? You won."

"Spoils to the victors, as they say. Me? I ain't spoiled enough. Your next word is *yes* or *no*. Did Yesenia cut a deal?"

It wasn't the answer I expected.

"No. That traitor made no deal."

If she wasn't such a dignified woman, I'm sure Evelyn would've hauled off and spit in my face. Privilege and social graces denied her the instinct, even now.

She chose honesty. Incredible.

The Senora knew those were possibly her last words, her final testament. She could've left this world with the satisfaction of having doomed Lumen to the same fate.

"Impressive, Senora. It's refreshing to discover people of great stature who don't hide behind obfuscation. I once knew an Empress who ruled seventeen planets in the name of a false god. She was a vulgar old coit, a woman who lived decades past her prime. But she didn't utter a false word. Even to the moment when I stabbed her through the heart, she was fearless. I respected her honesty."

Evelyn snarled at my little history lesson, which she must've considered a fantasy.

"Men like you respect no one."

"And therein lies the problem, Senora. You see, I'm not a man."

I reached inside to my syneth core, found the template of my original self, and shifted my form.

Damn, it hurt. Theo was right: I'd never return entirely to my old self. For now, however: I had the strength to become Royal again.

As my body reconfigured, Evelyn's defiance crumbled.

Now, I saw the terror.

What did she think of my original self? The bald scalp covered in a full tattoo of a red wolf. An Earth-born lab experiment raised on Hokkaido by parents of Earth-Asian descent. A serial killer, terrorist, enemy of the Swarm, universe jumper, immortal, slayer of species, savior of reality.

Eh. I didn't give a damn what she thought. Seeing was enough.

"My name is Royal, the wolf god."

Moon, who watched from the overturned sedan, transformed as well. He joined me for a celebratory moment. His barren scalp was covered in the tattooed scales of a serpent; and its head, fiery eyes, and fearsome jaws splayed across his face.

"I am Moon, the serpent god."

We hadn't seen each other this way since we fell to Azteca.

Time to finish our business.

"Is there anything you'd like me to say to your brother Mateo when I see him next? Or your children?"

"What ... are you?"

Oh. Well. That was a feeble response.

"We are what humans like you pretend to be. Except we've been around. And around. We'll still be around long after you people turn to dust. It's a nasty thought. Yes?"

I could've left her there, a miserable and defeated creature. No one would've believed her story. But in the event someone did, and word got back to the wrong folks in power ...

Yeah, no. We had too much work ahead to run afoul of the UNF or Q6, or whoever the hell wanted us dead.

Time for the next order of business.

I shot her in the head and transformed into Raul Torreta. My partner became Ilan Natchez again.

"That wasn't in the plan, my friend. Total improvisation. Brings back the memories. Yes?"

"The best."

I patted him on the shoulder.

"Thank you for letting me have her. I did agree for you to kill her at the ranch, but I was so caught up in the moment ..."

Moon reached retrieved his first cigar of the day, which he lit with the end of a finger. The cigar belonged to my partner's special stock.

"No worries, partner. You know how to make it right."

"I do. Now, I think our people are waiting on us."

At this point, I owed Moon many debts which I intended to pay as quickly as possible.

First, I needed intel. My pom contained the requested data relayed from Bart.

Keyword: Ixoca.

I threw open the results, which were surprisingly thin. I showed them to Moon, who took less fascination but understood the implication. He wanted satisfaction, and I intended to provide it.

When we arrived at the sedan, our team's celebration was muted. They knew this was an important victory but not the end of the war. They had loaded Harlan onboard.

We'd honor his sacrifice properly upon return.

"Any casualties in town?" I asked Elian.

"Just a pair of snakes."

"Plus many corpses beyond the perimeter."

"Eighty-four."

"Obviously, we'll face considerable cleanup."

Vash sat inside the door, holding a compress to his head.

"Elian, I'd like you to take everyone back to town. My partner and I have some matters to discuss with Vash."

Lumen's son perked up. How tight was the straitjacket now?

"Sure, boss," Elian said. "But we can't linger out here. What if the

184

wrong people show?"

"Not long, my friend. Jump back after five minutes."

"Gotcha, boss. Alright, everybody. Grab ahold of something. That first jump is a tummy-knocker."

"Vash," I said. "Join us please. We'd like to have a few words."

He did a nice job hiding the terror.

"Look, can we save it for later, Raul? I don't hardly remember what happened out there. My head is throbbing and ..."

"Sorry. Won't take long."

Moon helped him up and out.

The egress pixelated shut, and Moon led Vash into the field not far from where he laid Harlan. Bart lifted off and came about. A few seconds later, an aperture formed with the usual thunder and flash.

"First, I want to apologize, Vash."

He lowered the compress.

"For what?"

"The surprises. The secrets. We chose not to tell anyone but Elian about the worm drive. We made many illegal modifications, you see. In the wrong hands, well ...."

"You didn't trust me."

That was an understatement.

"We did get off to an awkward start."

Vash tried to play it cool.

"I thought I made it clear whose side I chose."

"Did you? Just this morning you told me that every day you still entertained thoughts of killing me."

"I was playing along with your dark humor, Raul. I meant nothing by it. If you had told me about the additional defense shield and the electrified zone between them, I would've supported the plan. It was a masterstroke to lure them in and ..."

"Fry them. Yes. It was genius. Thank Ilan. His idea."

Vash glanced at Moon, who hid any evidence of gloating.

"Well done, Ilan."

"Now, Vash, here's the real reason we need to talk: Ixoca."

"What?"

"When we boarded the train, Manny Borta said he wondered what happened to you after the trouble at Ixoca. You replied that it was too long a story. Remember?"

He stared at me like a half-wit. Or perhaps someone who saw no way out.

"What of it?"

"Ixoca does not exist on any map. It is neither business nor landmark. My exhaustive research found one obscure reference. An ancient term used by colonists who appeared to be the forefathers of the Children of Orpheus. It was a name they ascribed to an intelligence they believed visited shortly after they built a settlement in Ixtapa near the crash site of their Ark Carrier. Then the word vanished from all records. It's not even found in Aztecan literature. As if it had been scraped from existence. Odd, yes?"

He didn't give up, nor did he offer a defense.

"What do you want me to say, Raul?"

"Yes or no: *Ixoca* is a codeword among your cult. It has special meaning. In this case, Manny Borta letting you know that the plan to kill my partner and me was in place."

"What plan?"

"Simple yes or no, Vash."

"You already know the answer."

"I do."

I'd been wrong twice this day. The first mistake almost claimed my life. The second was pinning it on a Lumen-Vash double team.

"I must give you credit, Vash. The night your people arrived to train the militia, you told me that I wouldn't have the element of surprise on my side next time. I didn't take you seriously. I thought you learned your lesson. But damned if you didn't hide a nifty surprise in broad daylight.

"You're far more connected than I realized. You cut a deal with

186

Evelyn Cardinale. Used your Orpheus contacts in the shipping industry and made sure a longtime ally audited the products in hold three. What was the plan for the town and your mother?"

Now would've been a good time to piss his pants. Instead, Vash found his manhood and stood tall.

"No one would've been touched. Only you two and Elian. Others can cook Motif."

"Ah. And what of the invaders? I assume they would've disarmed the militia and controlled the town until everyone understood their place in the new order."

"No, Raul. The old order. Mother's order."

There he was. A steel-jawed, thick-spined assassin ready for whatever fate had in store.

I laughed. "Ironic. Lumen had no idea, did she?"

"I wanted to surprise her."

What could a fallen god do but take his lumps and move on? I genuinely thought Vash might become a reasonable ally someday.

"Yes, my friend. She will be surprised."

I glanced aside, caught the twinkle in Moon's eyes, and nodded.

Moon took care of business faster than I sighed.

His cigar's weaponized fire burned a hole into Vash's cheek. No one else would hear the screams.

The fire bore deep and treated his body like kindling.

Vash Rodriguez found a home. His ashes would help nourish these lovely fields.

A tragedy, I reckon.

The asshole messed around and found out: Don't fuck with gods.

A moment later, Bart returned.

"Two for home," I said with an air of victory.

Elian saw who was missing and grinned. Yes, he was going to be an outstanding lieutenant.

"Gotcha, boss."

21

T HE FULL MILITIA GAVE US a hero's welcome. While it posed an opportunity to bask in the glory – and I enjoyed a healthy share of adulation poured on thick – the business of tributes and farewells would have to wait. We shook hands with the faithful, but I avoided a speech. Important business filled my plate.

"A round of drinks," I announced. "Elian's buying."

Elian feigned shock but quickly recognized the honor I bestowed.

"Thanks, boss. No one's ever trusted me like you did today."

"You delivered, my friend. I'll never ask for more. Oh, and here's a tip. One delightful way to earn friends and followers: Fill their bellies with liquor on your credits."

Elian extended his hand, which I received. A firmer grip I'd never encountered – outside of my partner, of course.

"I'll buy a round for the whole town, boss. And it won't be the last. What we did today is just the beginning."

"Page one." I lowered my voice even though the crowd was dispersing toward the cantina. "By the way, what did you do with Oria and Den?"

"Oh, shit. Those malgados. I dumped them in Bart's wardrobe. It was a tight fit, but I had to work fast."

A fitting end for Vash's lieutenants.

"No worries." I lent a side-eye to Moon. "We'll handle them. Go inside and celebrate, Elian. You earned it."

"Thanks, boss." He extended his hand to Moon. "And thank *you*, boss. Maybe I haven't said it, but you inspire me, Ilan."

Moon, ever the socially inept, fumbled the compliment with a pitiful handshake and a crooked smile.

"We're happy you're on our team, Elian."

A tad stiff, but not bad.

When our lieutenant retreated toward the cantina, dancing on air, I couldn't help but chuckle.

"Don't look now, my friend, but you have a protégé."

Moon grunted. "He still has a long way to go."

"True. Some loose edges to polish. You can help him grow."

"I'm not a teacher."

"Two thousand years of backstory says otherwise. It's time for him to learn exactly what we are. Take him with you to clean up the perimeter tonight. Offer him a cigar. Special stock. Teach him about syneth. Absolute trust must be earned, Moon."

"And if he can't handle the truth?"

"He will."

"If not?"

"Make him. I'm fond of that young man."

Moon's groan said he wasn't looking forward to the task, but my partner needed a healthy opportunity to bond with a human.

"Hmmph. You want me to make friends with these people. You want me to think of this place as home."

"Wouldn't hurt, my friend. And as I've said many times, nothing we do here suggests permanence. We'll leave Azteca for greener worlds before long."

Moon turned his eyes toward the cantina and the one person who had leaned against the wall since we stepped off Bart.

"She will never be a friend."

189

"You're right," I said, staring at Lumen. "But what she will be remains an open question. If you don't mind, I'd like to handle this bit myself."

"All yours. I need a drink. I'm thirsty. Without my reserves ..."

"Understood. It's going to be an adjustment for us both."

We'd have to discuss what happened on the train and how it affected our future, but now was not the time.

I began crafting my strategy for Lumen the moment I knew we'd have to kill her son. There was an easy route and a hard one. In Lumen's case, I preferred the latter. In the long term, it benefited our goals and Desperido.

The choice belonged to Lumen.

She ignored Moon as he passed her. Typical. When she saw I did not intend to follow, she beat a hesitant path toward me. Her fists were balled at her side, no overt sign of a weapon.

She was a smart woman. She had to know. Yet a mother held out hope, or so I assumed.

I correctly predicted her first question.

"Where is he?"

I pointed south.

"We should take a walk."

"No. Where is Vash?"

Perhaps I could've played games or been my usual flippant self, but the moment required a different touch.

"I'm an open book, but you have to walk with me."

I turned my back and strutted into the desert. The risk was negligible. Shooting me in the back wasn't the answer.

So, she followed.

"Now. Tell me, Raul."

"Your son betrayed everyone, Lumen. Me, Ilan, our team, Elian, this town. And by extension ... you."

"Vash is not ..."

"A traitor? Not in his heart. He believed he was doing right by

190

everyone. He struck a deal with the Horax, planted assassins onboard the road train, and intended to free Desperido of its new owners." I walked and talked, oblivious to her expression. "The Horax used professionals it embedded inside Montez Shipping. They failed. At that point, the deal collapsed. The Horax were willing to cripple the train, kill everyone inside, steal our products, and assault this town. His lieutenants, Oria and Den, were charged with murdering Elian and lowering the defense perimeter.

"What he did not understand was that the Horax had no intention of following through with their end of the deal. They would've killed you, slaughtered most of our contractors, and kidnapped the most valuable to work for them elsewhere. He put everyone at risk merely to impress his mother."

I gave her a moment to process her son's last foolish (albeit potentially shrewd) endeavor. She grabbed me by the shoulder and swung me about – only because I allowed it.

"You are a bastard and a liar. Vash would never go behind me to put my life's work at risk."

She said the words like she meant them, but I heard the doubt.

"It wasn't about you, Lumen. He was selfish. He wanted to surprise you. His words, not mine."

"You're lying. Even if he did these things, my son wouldn't waste his breath confessing to you."

I resumed my walk. One aspect of the desert I appreciated: Silence.

"I knew the truth before I confronted him. The only blank left to fill in: Whether *you* were complicit. I now know you weren't. Care to guess how?"

"Stop skirting past it, Raul. Where is Vash?"

No. Not yet.

"Do you know who led the operation against us?"

"Answer me."

"She was there, Lumen."

"Stop playing games."

"In retrospect, she made her position clear to you. The great Senora said there was no compensation fit for her losses. Her sympathy was as dry as the desert you called home. I remember how she finished the message: 'Time lays waste to all hope.'" I wagged a finger. "Now that, my friend, is a woman bent on maximum slaughter. Fortunately, I asked her one question before I killed her. Evelyn Cardinale gave you a pass."

I continued walking, but with no one at my side. When I swung around, Lumen froze in place, a quiet sentinel who realized I might not be lying.

For a change.

"You're free, Lumen. Free of the arrangement forced upon you thirty years ago. I doubt she told anyone the truth about Vash's father. And after I adjust a few levers, the Horax as an entity will never bother this town again."

On any other day, she might've shown relief. But Lumen damn well knew I was about to drop the other proverbial shoe. Still, I pushed my case.

"There's a collusion – expansive, I suspect – between the cartels and the shipping industry. The Horax have been severely weakened. We can press our advantage and set their nearest rivals against the Horax. They'll fight each other, we'll use your contacts within the Children of Orpheus, and Desperido's secret economy will expand. There's a big, wide victory to be had."

OK, so I made a huge promise I wasn't certain to keep. We were likely to draw scrutiny in the coming days, but if Road Train 1492's Navs spoke up, Nestor and Bett might shift attention to the much bigger fish.

"You're certain she's dead?"

"Yes, Lumen. Not only is Evelyn Cardinale deceased, but she died in great pain. You'd wish for nothing less."

The lump in her throat expanded.

192

"And Vash?"

"What choice did we have? We killed him."

There went those fists again. Oh, to pound me senseless.

Lumen, being a woman with an iceberg of a heart, did not attack. She choked out her next question.

"Where?"

"He'll never be found."

Lumen flared her nostrils and slitted her eyes but shed no tears. I knew then she was mine if I got her through the day.

"I wish his plan had worked," she said.

"No doubt. However, you'd be dealing with a far more sinister opponent than me; but sure, it might've been worth the tradeoff."

"What now? Am I next?"

"Had you conspired against us? Oh, yes. But given that this town is your home and your legacy, I have no desire to harm you. Same goes for Ilan. You can walk the path alongside us. You can leave this town a liberated woman. The choice is yours."

"Choice. Is that what you gave my son?"

"No. Vash knew he was a dead man long before we killed him. That's the life of an assassin, you see. Death haunts the parties on both ends. And I should remind you: Vash survived until today by sheer luck of the draw. He would be alive if you had never tried to assassinate us in the first place. Causality is a nasty mistress, and no one in this universe knows more about causality than I."

Her unibrow flexed. I had learned its many curves and contortions. This one signaled confusion and curiosity.

Best she didn't explore further. She was not prepared for the truth.

"After everything, you'd allow me to stay here. The man who killed my son doesn't think I'd come after him again."

"You won't. It's futile."

"Any man can be killed, Raul."

"In theory. Lumen, consider these points. Tomorrow will be your first full day as a free woman. You'll wake many pounds lighter. In time, you'll understand the depth of Vash's betrayal and decide to leave the past behind. You have influential connections. My partner and I are resourceful in ways that would boggle the ordinary mind. An alliance of convenience is not beyond reason."

We walked amid the sagebrush, leaving heavy footprints in the thick red dust. Lumen wouldn't dare say it, but the deal made financial sense.

"What's your price, Raul?"

Nice. I knew she had it in her to think past her loss.

"Only what I previously asked. Now that you're free from the Horax threat, you owe me a full disclosure about the Children of Orpheus. We'll start with a single word I learned today: Ixoca."

I didn't wait for a reaction. Between her grief and her rage, Lumen was difficult to read.

"Vash and his Orpheus collaborator used it. It's a code word among your group, but I believe it's so much more. It's a word your people all but erased from the Aztecan historical data spools. What possible motive? I wonder."

Lumen smashed a foot into the ground, kicking a dust cloud into my face.

"You'll never let it rest. Will you?"

I feigned a cough.

"I'm nothing if not persistent. But I also like to think I'm fair." After a shrug, I added: "Sleep on it. We'll discuss over breakfast tomorrow. The first day Desperido reports to no outside masters."

She turned on her heels.

"There's always a master, Raul."

I would've said, "You're talking to one."

Yeah, no. That seemed a tad narcissistic, so I bit my lip.

Lumen trudged toward town to confront her choices. Who would've blamed her had she walked away? If she stayed – an outcome I expected – she didn't have to walk arm in arm with the men who ruined every facet of her life. But she would remain in close proximity.

As I told Moon hours later, we needed Lumen.

For now.

Something about the Children of Orpheus piqued my curiosity beyond the norm. They were no mere cult. Religious fanatics and extremists rose and fell by the generation; these folks kept their eyes on the prize for centuries *and* remained hidden in clear view.

Must have been one hell of a prize.

Intuition said they had a role to play in our dream of creating an interstellar criminal empire.

"It's been a long journey, my friend," I told Moon as we watched the sunset from the town's western perimeter. "Mine almost ended on that train."

Moon exhaled a thin, disciplined stream of cigar smoke.

"I never saw you like that before, Royal."

"Like what?"

"Frightened."

"Was I? It all happened so fast."

"How did you overlook it? You don't make mistakes."

I stifled a laugh.

"Oh, I've made plenty, most before you entered my lives."

"Their strategy wasn't hard to spot. I suspected Vash and Manny from the first."

"Huh. And you said nothing because you assumed ..."

"You should have seen it coming, Royal. I warned you."

"When?"

"I said you'll meet a human who will be three steps ahead, and you won't know until you lose."

It all came back to me. The day I described my grand vision for taking over Desperido, Moon spotted trouble on the horizon. Now, the tense lines above his brow suggested a deeper fear.

Huh. Theo warned me, too. He said Vash would hit me from my

blind spot.

"You think I'm losing my edge?"

"It's this town. These people are ordinary. Yeah, a few have potential. Elian, maybe. Ship? Someday. But Royal, we aren't meant to rub shoulders with the ordinary. We need others like us."

I smirked. "Fallen gods?"

He scoffed. "Don't be a cunt. You know what I mean. We don't belong in civilized society."

"It's true. They tend to frown on murder and mayhem. Desperido is a nice fit for the short term."

"You're a stubborn ass. You almost died, and I almost lost the only friend I've known for two thousand years."

I didn't ignore the sense of urgency in his tone. He didn't ask, "What would I have done on my own?" But I heard the fear.

Moon didn't care about giving up his syneth reserves. He'd pull from his core if it meant keeping me alive. "Civilized society" did not need Moon walking about as a free agent, and my partner damn well knew it.

"I apologize, my friend. Today's oversight marked a blip on an otherwise spectacular record. I'll study on how to avoid such a trap ever again."

"Don't bullshit me, Royal. You won't give it another thought."

Yep. My partner knew me inside and out.

"We won, Moon. All quality battles are fought at the edges. We cut it close but prevailed. Many more battles lay ahead. We'll win them, too. The future is written, my friend. We saw it in the timeline. Minor setbacks will not deter us. Trust me."

I winked. "I got this."

He blew smoke in my face. Well deserved.

"It's time to clean up the mess out there. Sure you don't want to join me?"

"Incineration is your gig, Moon. I'll leave you to it. But I had a thought. Why don't you hunt down Ship and bring him along? He already knows we're different. Might as well show him the rest."

"Whatever you say, partner."

"Perfect. Our lieutenants should know they're working for gods."

Moon grumbled as he left. I still had that effect on him, even after two millennia.

Truth was, I wanted to be alone.

Moon was right. I allowed a human to get ahead of me. It was inexcusable. The next time I screwed up would be my last.

I stood there until long after the sun's light disappeared and cursed until my pity party ran out of steam.

Then I pulled myself together, opened my flask, and imbibed my favorite whiskey.

"Onto the next battle, my friend."

A soft melody echoed through my mind. My *D'ru-shaya* returned.

"Cheers," Theo said. *"Don't listen to the naysayers, Royal. You know what's best for everyone."*

Huh.

OK, so that was Theo, more or less. The voice was male, but the tone was uncomfortably soft. Not a hint of disrespect.

Even a tad ...

Oh, shit. Feminine.

"Theo?"

"Hi, buddy."

"Theo, what happened to Addis? Did you remove her echo?"

He giggled.

Like a schoolgirl.

"Oh. That. Well, what happened was, you see, the reserves affected my operational matrix. Addis is very loud. I tried to remove her. I did, Royal. Honest."

"What happened, Theo? Where's Addis?"

A woman intervened with a full-throated shout.

"I'm here, Royal! We both are."

"Which means what exactly?"

"*There wasn't a choice.*" I heard a masculine response. "*I couldn't dispose of her, old man.*"

"*Please don't tell me you ...*"

Wild clapping ensued, then the softer voice.

"*We merged, Royal. Isn't it just the best? I'm teaching Theo how to be kinder and gentler. Once we're fully assimilated, you'll experience the best of both D'ru-shayas. Aren't you excited?*"

I missed Theo's nasty demeanor already.

"*This is unacceptable. I will not have two D'ru-shayas in my ear.*"

"*Actually,*" the male voice said, "*Addis is right. I thought I'd hate sharing a space with her melodramatic baggage, but she's actually quite endearing when you get to know her. I could see a time when we might fall in love.*"

"*You're not serious.*"

"*I am. Dumbass.*" Theo chuckled. "*That one was for old time's sake. I was an awful prude, wasn't I? Anyhow, we thought to pay you a quick visit before we return to our assimilation. We'll keep to ourselves for a while. If you need me in a pinch, of course I'll respond. But I'd rather you mind your own business for the time being. Have a lovely evening, Royal.*"

Huh.

They expected me to listen to that until the end of time?

Yeah, no.

I retreated to the cantina, where a tall bottle of whiskey awaited.

What is Ixoca? How does it connect to the Children of Orpheus? Will a tenuous alliance between Raul and Lumen hold long enough for the truth to be unveiled? Can Desperido continue to thrive after the road train attack? Will the violence attract unwanted attention from those searching for Royal and Moon?

Continue "Gods & Assassins" now in Book 3: *Blue Heart*. The entire series is available on Amazon.

Printed in Great Britain
by Amazon